OHIO
DOMINICAN
UNIVERSITY™

SINCE 1911

ALSO BY PAT DERBY

Goodbye Emily, Hello
Grams, Her Boyfriend, My Family, and Me
Visiting Miss Pierce

AWAY TO THE GOLDFIELDS!

ERBY

Away to the Goldfields!

FARRAR, STRAUS AND GIROUX

NEW YORK

www.fsgkidsbooks.com

Library of Congress Cataloging-in-Publication Data
Derby, Pat.
    Away to the goldfields! / Pat Derby.— 1st ed.
        p. cm.
    Summary: Yearning for adventure and tired of farm life in New
Hampshire, sixteen-year-old Mary Margaret Malarkey journeys to
California in 1848 to find her father who arrived earlier to make his
fortune in the goldfields.
    ISBN 0-374-39961-1
    [1. Voyages and travels—Fiction.   2. Adventure and adventurers—Fiction.
3. California—Gold discoveries—Fiction.   4. California—History—1846–
1850—Fiction.]   I. Title.

PZ7.D4415Aw 2004
[Fic]—dc22

                                                                    2003064217

To my next generation of readers:
Ryan, Jeff, Megan, Kate Padilla, and Brittany Derby

AWAY TO THE GOLDFIELDS!

Prologue

Mary Margaret Murphy braced herself against the ship's rail. She hugged her shawl, feeling the sharp salt spray prick her cheek. Occasionally the ends of the shawl whipped across her face. She would absently pull them away, her eyes focused on the fast-receding shoreline.

"Good riddance," she whispered. She leaned forward, resting her arms on the railing, feeling the push and pull of the water vibrating through the wood.

"It's a sad thing, watching your home fade away," Nathan Winthrop, the first mate, said. He had been watching her for a while. Of all the sad refugees who had straggled aboard in Dublin, she was the one to catch his eye. He had liked the way she carried herself, head held high, almost running up the gangplank. She was followed by a young man who could only be her brother. They both had the same glorious mop of red hair, but whereas she radiated health, the brother was pale and walked with a hesitating step. They had carried what appeared to be all their belongings in a frayed carpetbag and several parcels wrapped in brown paper. Nathan had not been surprised to find their ticket marked steerage, destination Boston.

Mary Margaret turned to face the first mate. "Shall I be honest?" she asked.

Nathan hesitated. He had expected a more maidenly shyness, or perhaps a few tears tracking down the rosy cheeks or a shy dropping of her glance. Instead, Mary Margaret boldly maintained eye contact.

"Well, of course," he said.

" 'Tis no great loss to me," she said. "I understand it's a fine new land we're going to where a person's station and religion are of no concern. And that there is land free for the taking."

Nathan laughed. He was charmed. What an enchanting creature, he thought. So much more colorful than the pale New England girls with their somber gray dresses, gentle voices, and quiet manners. This Irish lass was dressed roughly, no doubt of that. Her dress was made of the coarsest material, and she had on what appeared to be her brother's outgrown shoes. But peeking out from her skirts was the slash of a crimson petticoat, and the hair that the shawl inadequately covered curled in a charming helter-skelter manner around her face.

"Where is your brother?" Nathan asked. He didn't respond to her remark about the nature of America because he didn't want to dim the excitement in her eyes.

"Michael hasn't the stomach for the sea," Mary Margaret said. "At least I hope that's his problem. There was so much fever about before we left. Half of Dublin was sickening. And we buried Da just last week."

"I'm sorry," Nathan said. "I can see why you're anxious to make a fresh start."

Mary Margaret turned back to gaze at the horizon. "We didn't have much choice," she said. "There was a price on Da's head, and we were afraid they would come for Michael." She hesitated. "It's true, it is hard to leave, but at least we're safe."

Nathan made a reassuring gesture. There was no point in telling her what America was really like. Land free for the taking, indeed! He had walked the meaner streets of Boston, and he knew that the life of a refugee was anything but easy.

Three months later Mary Margaret Murphy walked alone down the gangplank into the maelstrom of Boston's wharf. She was carrying the carpetbag and the paper packages, now torn and dirty. She wasn't sure what she would do with her brother's clothes, but it would be foolish to let the sailors steal them. She didn't trust them, even though that first mate Nathan had been kind. No, he had been more than that, she admitted to herself. She knew he cared about her. He had made sure that a Catholic sailor had read the service when Michael's body slipped from under a flag and disappeared into the sea, and he had always seen that she had enough to eat. She suspected he had even taken food from the sailors' mess to give to her.

Nathan came up behind her and touched her lightly on the shoulder. "Will you return home?" he asked.

Mary Margaret shook her head. "Not likely," she said.

"But what will you do?"

"I'll get by," she said.

"In that case," Nathan said, "I had better take you home with me."

Mary Margaret nodded.

Pa didn't even want me to go to school. The only reason I can read and write and cipher is because he wanted his six boys to be able to so that nobody could cheat them. Malachi, who was a year and a half older than me, wouldn't go to school when he was little. He complained that he couldn't understand the teacher and that all those letters and numbers looked like chicken scratches to him. Besides, he whispered to Ma, he was scared there all alone.

So Pa let me go with Malachi. I loved school and I loved to read. Sometimes the teacher, Mr. Fulton, would lend me books, and then Ma would sit in her rocker and I would sit on the stool next to her and we would read together. We never did that when Pa was around. He would get angry when he saw us just doing nothing, and he would bang around the kitchen demanding food or water, anything to make Ma stop reading and get up.

Ma died when I was twelve. Pa said all that thinking and reading weakened her brain and that was why she died. Reading didn't kill her. If you ask me, she died from Pa being so nasty and from having six boys and me and two babies that never lived long enough for the priest to get to the house and baptize them. She told me once that she baptized them herself with the washing-up water. Ma was gentle and sweet and never raised her voice. Pa wasn't nice to her or to any of us kids for that matter. Ma cooked and tended the animals on our poor, rocky New Hampshire farm, and she couldn't hold her head up because Pa owed everybody in

Ma always said I reminded her of her mother, Gra
Winthrop. That's why she named me Mary Margaret.
Pa heard that, he would grunt and say Grandma w
most uppity woman he ever knew. I never met Gra
Winthrop. Ma told me Grandma was only sixteen, ju
age, when she traveled to America and that she had t
my mother all alone after Nathan Winthrop, her hu
went down in a big storm off the Newfoundland coast
were only married for two years. She bought a fishin
with the money she got when Grandpa Winthrop die
she hired a young man to take it out. She made e
money to buy a little house of her own. Ma said Gra
prided herself on being independent and beholden
one. Pa said it was unnatural, and that women shoul
to things like washing and cooking.

town. He was so mean that even when the shopkeepers were willing to wait on the money, Pa would cheat them anyway.

I think Ma died because she was tired. One spring morning, instead of starting the vegetable patch, she just went quietly back to bed and never woke up. After we buried her, I gathered up Grandma's quilt, which had come from County Sligo with her, and claimed a rocker that had belonged to Grandpa's mother, before Pa could try to sell it.

With Ma gone, Pa decided that whatever Malachi hadn't learned by then—and believe me, he hadn't learned much—he never would, and so Pa made Malachi leave school. I had to quit too. The schoolmaster tried to convince Pa to let me stay on so someday I could become a schoolmarm, but Pa said, "I don't want no snotty girl laughing at her old pa behind his back, thinking she was smarter than me. No, sir, she'll stay home and be a good daughter the way the good Lord meant her to."

I began to worry that Pa would insist I marry some big lumbering farmer just like him, and then I'd never get to leave this miserable town and I'd end up like Ma. Only I wouldn't be sweet and gentle. I never understood how she kept her thoughts to herself. Ma tried to tell me that it did no good to argue with Pa because that only made him madder. Even when I tried to keep quiet, words just fell out of my mouth. Pa had never hit Ma, but he often beat my brothers, and he would whack me. I guess that's why some of my brothers left when I was little. Ma said she missed them, but she didn't blame them for going. This wasn't a good life for them.

And then in March of 1848 Harry Throckmorton, our neighbor, came bursting into our cabin. Pa, my brothers Malachi and Matt, and I were just finishing dinner.

"Murray," Harry Throckmorton said to Pa, "what do you think this is?" He opened the small sack he was carrying.

Pa fingered the shiny dust spilling from the sack onto my clean kitchen table. "Funny-colored sand?" he said.

"Gold!" Mr. Throckmorton said.

Pa laughed. "Somebody's pulling your leg."

"No, it's gold! From California. That's where my cousin Phil found it. He says it's just lying there in the rivers. It don't belong to nobody. A fellow can just pick it up and wouldn't be arrested or anything like that." Harry Throckmorton rubbed his hands together. "And my cousin Phil says there ain't many people know about it yet either. He says if we had even the brains God gave a woman, why, we should get ourselves out there in a hurry."

"I don't believe you can just pick it up from the river," I said. "Why would your cousin tell you? Why wouldn't he gather it all up for himself?"

"Now, missy," Mr. Throckmorton replied, "that's not anything you should worry about." He winked and nudged my father. "She never would understand about what it takes to make a trip like that."

Pa looked puzzled. "I never heard you had a cousin."

"He's in the army," Mr. Throckmorton said. "Sent me this and told me to get my hide out there soon as I could. Now I tell you, Murray," Mr. Throckmorton continued, "forget this miserable farm. What is it? Nothing but rocks. How much have you saved for all the years you've lived here? Nothing, I bet. And nothing to leave your kids. Come with me. We'll be rich."

"Where's this Californy?" Matt asked.

"Out west," Mr. Throckmorton said. "As far as you can go. And when you get to the end, why, there's California and the ocean. Leastways that's what Phil says."

"What I don't understand," I said, "is if there's gold just lying around, why don't other people know about it? I would think millions of people would be out there picking it up."

"Now there she's right," Mr. Throckmorton said. "We can't waste any time. This won't stay a secret for long."

Pa picked up a few specks of gold and let them run through his fingers. "I'll do it! I'll go. I never did like farming. A man can't earn a decent living always worrying about the weather. One year it's too hot and the next it's too cold. No, sir, Murray Malarkey was never born to be a farmer!"

It was news to me that he had ever thought of himself as a farmer. Ma and then me had been the ones to plant and nurse the vegetable patch and tend to the chickens. To be honest, our farm was made up of mostly thin, rocky soil where practically nothing grew. Without the eggs we sold, the milk from our cow, and Pa renting out our two horses, Toby and Ben, we wouldn't have had any money coming in.

It wasn't much of a life, and I wasn't surprised that Pa would want to leave. He had never shown any interest in the farm—or in his family, as far as that went. Pa had promised Ma a house, but our cabin was a sorry mess. It had one big room. Ma had curtained off a corner to make a sleeping place for her and Pa. In another corner was the sink and pump and the pantry. We cooked in the fireplace. The boys slept in the tumbledown barn in the summer and up in the attic in the winter. After my older brothers left, I slept in the attic alone.

I couldn't believe I would be getting out of this town. "When will we go?" I asked. "And what will we do with the farm?"

Pa swept the dust back into the leather bag and handed it to Mr. Throckmorton. He glared at me. "I'm not dragging a passel of kids along to this here Californy," he said.

My brother Malachi was eighteen; Matt, the only other brother still at home, was twenty-one; and I was sixteen. I didn't think we could be considered a passel of kids.

Before I could open my mouth to protest, my father continued: "On the other hand, Matt here has a strong back and knows when to keep quiet. I'll take him."

"Why can't I go too?" Malachi demanded.

"Because you're stupid," Matt said.

"Because we can't burn all our bridges," Pa said. "Now, I'm not saying we won't find gold, but it makes no sense to just leave the farm. No, Malachi, you stay here and watch after Molly, and when Matt and I hit it big, why, we'll send for you. If anything goes wrong, find your older brothers. Can't say I know where they are, though."

"Take us all," I said. "Malachi can dig for gold as good as Matt, and I can cook and wash for you. I can dig too. I dig up the vegetable garden every year."

"Don't talk nonsense. You and Malachi will stay here and tend the place and do as you're told." Pa winked at Mr. Throckmorton. "They're plenty old enough to take care of themselves. Seems to me it's about time Molly here should be thinking of getting hitched. Instead she wants to go to Californy? I tell you, it ain't going to be easy finding her a husband. No man wants an uppity female."

"Well, really," I said. I flounced out the door and would have slammed it, but it hung crooked and wouldn't shut properly. I stood outside the cabin, struggling to get a hold of my temper.

"Don't you be sulking, miss," Pa shouted at me through the half-closed door. "Just you start gathering up my clothes and packing us enough food for the journey."

In a week Pa and Matt and Mr. Throckmorton were gone. One morning when I woke up, I found they had left. Pa and Matt didn't even say goodbye. I figured he didn't want any more arguments from me. They never told us how they were getting to California or how long they would be gone. A few days later, when I went to fetch the butter and egg money to buy more feed for my chickens, I found that Pa had taken it. In truth, he had taken almost everything that was worth anything, including the blankets and the food stored in the pantry.

I went looking for Malachi. It wasn't easy finding him anymore. In a way I didn't blame him. Even I had been seized with a sense of freedom without Pa around. But I hadn't stopped doing what I was supposed to do. I still got up early to feed the chickens and our remaining horse, Ben. Pa had taken Toby, the other horse, with him. I guess he planned to sell him to get money. Malachi, though, had been behaving like a little kid. I was out of bed before sunup but he would sleep to almost seven, and he hardly did any work at all. Of course, there wasn't much to do until the ground thawed. Sometimes then a local farmer might hire him to help with the planting. By late afternoon he would be gone. I think he was with some of those Grisson boys. Even Pa said those boys couldn't be trusted.

Malachi would wander home at all hours. One night I woke up and heard him banging around, tripping over chairs, dropping the metal water dipper on the floor. For a minute, before I was fully awake, I thought Pa was home. As I snuggled down under Grandma's quilt, I thought, I'm glad it's Malachi even if he does sound like he's been drinking. I wouldn't say that Malachi was outright thick in the head, but he sure wasn't smart, and he certainly had a hankering for running with the wrong sort. But he had been such a sweet little boy, I couldn't help but care about him. Besides, Ma had always said that if anything happened to her, I should watch out for Malachi.

With Pa taking the little bit of money we had and the chicken feed running out, I needed to go to Mr. Hawkins's general store. I put on my bonnet and gathered the eggs into a basket.

"Hello, Molly," Mr. Hawkins greeted me when I got to his store. "Have you heard anything from your pa?" He lifted my basket onto his counter. "I haven't seen you about lately, but I've seen Malachi." He shook his head. "That boy is certainly acting foolish, gambling and drinking every night."

Like Ma, I didn't believe in parading our family's dirty linen, and Lord knows we have plenty. "I'm sure Malachi will settle down," I said. "How much will you give me for these eggs?"

"Well now, Molly. Your pa owed me a parcel. He hasn't paid his bill for over six months."

I gulped. I never dreamed our bills were so overdue. "Mr. Hawkins, I need money to buy feed for the chickens. If the chickens aren't fed, I won't have any eggs to sell."

"You're a nice girl, Molly. I always liked you and your ma, but I'm not a rich man. I've got twelve mouths to feed, what with Peggy and that husband of hers and the young'un she's expecting. And there's just you and your brother now, and I can't say I'm much impressed with Malachi. Strikes me he's a chip off the old block. I know you mean well, but . . ." He shrugged his shoulders. "I can't see how I'll ever get paid."

I reached for my basket, but Mr. Hawkins laid a heavy hand on it. "I'll just add these up and take them off the bill." His smile reminded me of Pa's. I couldn't blame Cyrus Hawkins, though. His kids weren't dressed any better than anyone else's. It wasn't easy making a living in this town.

He handed me back my empty basket. "If you need money, old Miss Berryman is always looking for a healthy girl to help her."

He went to pat my hand, but I pulled away, gave him a sharp look, and marched out. Almost every poor girl in town, at one time or another, had worked for Miss Berryman. She didn't want a day girl. She wanted somebody there morning, noon, and night, always at her beck and call. My friend Lucy worked for Miss Berryman now. But I suspected not for long. Lucy told me Miss Berryman would wake her up in the middle of the night to get her a drink of water or, even worse, to empty her chamber pot!

"I think she wants to be sure I'm still in the house," Lucy complained. "I'm not crazy. Why would I meet some boy outside in the middle of winter? And she counts the eggs and potatoes to make sure I'm not eating too much."

I stood in front of Mr. Hawkins's store. I was so angry I couldn't think. All I knew was that I was not going to run and fetch for Miss Berryman or anyone like her. I pulled my shawl tighter around my shoulders and, with the empty basket banging against my ankles, marched back toward our farm. Ma's grave was out back along with the graves of the two babies who hadn't really lived at all. Whenever I felt lonely or angry, I went out there to talk to her.

"I know you're in heaven, Ma, if anybody is," I said, staring down at the snow that hid Ma's grave. "See if you can't talk to some of them saints up there in heaven with you. Get them on my side."

I scraped the snow off the grave, pulled a few branches over, and laid them near the cross. I didn't like how cold her grave looked in winter. I ran my finger along the splintering wood of the cross. "But don't fret, Ma. I'll be okay. You just enjoy your rest with all them angels."

When I got back to the house, I went down to the root cellar. Fortunately, Pa hadn't looked there. I figured there were enough potatoes and winter vegetables so that Malachi and I wouldn't starve. The chickens would just have to peck for food, and I could let the cow out to pasture even if there was still snow on the ground. When things were completely thawed, I'd be able to plant the vegetable garden. Maybe Malachi could hire himself out. Just as I had told Pa, Malachi could dig just fine. I hoped the way he had been acting the last few weeks, making a fool of himself and all, wouldn't stop someone from hiring him. I gathered up a few potatoes and took them to the kitchen.

I hadn't told Malachi about the food stored in the cellar. I was afraid if he thought we had enough, he wouldn't even look for work. Instead, I told him that Pa hadn't left us much of anything, which was true enough. At dinner that night I told him he had better think about finding a farmer who needed an extra hand.

"I know what they'll want me to do," Malachi said. "I'll have to move boulders. I hate moving boulders."

"Can't be helped," I said. "Pa left us nothing to live on."

Malachi muttered something at me as he left. I smiled. Maybe if he was out in some fields, he wouldn't have time to see those Grisson boys. Don't worry, Ma, I said under my breath. I'll take care of Malachi and the farm too. You don't have to fret about us none.

2

"Mr. Hawkins says there's a letter for you," Lucy said. It was September and we hadn't heard anything from Pa and Matt since they left. Lucy had seated herself on a boulder and was watching me hoe the vegetable plot. She always said she was my best friend, and since she was my only friend, I guess she was. Right about the time Ma died and Pa made me leave school, Lucy's ma kept her out of school to help with the younger children. Whenever she could get away, she would wander over to our farm and talk to me. But all she wanted to do was gossip about boys and who was sweet on who. She didn't seem to mind at all that she wasn't going to school. "I never was much interested in book learning," she told me.

I pushed Pa's old straw hat back on my head and wiped

the sweat out of my eyes. "How'd you get away from Miss Berryman today?" I asked.

Lucy shrugged. "I'm shopping." Then she giggled. "Aren't you curious about the letter?"

Of course I was. But Lucy couldn't keep her mouth shut, and it wasn't anybody's business what Pa was up to. I wouldn't have been surprised if he was broke and writing to ask us for money. As if we had any money.

"I have to finish with the vegetables," I said.

Lucy stood up and straightened the tie on her sunbonnet. "Well, if I was you, I'd be crazy to find out who was writing me a letter. Maybe it's from your pa. Maybe he's found gold!"

"Maybe," I replied. "But I'm not sure Pa can even write."

"Let's go down to Mr. Hawkins's store and see what it is," Lucy coaxed. "I'll tell Miss Berryman I was helping a friend."

"I'll go later," I said. I didn't want Lucy there when Mr. Hawkins reminded me of all the money Pa owed. After a few more minutes she shrugged her shoulders and told me she couldn't risk standing around in the sun getting freckles, because boys didn't like freckles.

I watched her go down the dirt road before I went over to the pump. I washed the dust off my hands and shook out my skirt. I didn't hurry because I knew that around three o'clock Mr. Hawkins let one of his young'uns mind the store while he went home for a quick nap. If I was lucky, I could get my letter when he wasn't there.

I thought about what Malachi and I were going to do if Pa didn't come home soon. We had enough food now, but I didn't know what we would do during the winter. I could preserve or dry some of our produce, except at the rate Malachi bolted his food, there wouldn't be much left over to store. Besides, our egg production had gone down since I could only let the chickens scratch for their food.

When I got to town, I saw that Mr. Hawkins was still behind the counter at his store, so I wandered down the street and looked at the school. It had been closed for most of the summer and wouldn't open again until the harvest was in. I sighed. It seemed a long time since I had been there. There's no point wishing for what I can't have, I told myself. Finally I turned and headed back to the store. I was glad to see Mr. Hawkins's daughter Peggy behind the counter. I pushed open the door.

"Molly, I haven't seen much of you lately," Peggy said.

"I've been busy," I replied. "Lucy says you have a letter for me?"

"Pa didn't say anything. Let me look around." She started rummaging around the counter where Mr. Hawkins sold stamps and accepted things to be mailed. "This place is such a mess. Sometimes I think my father is getting too old to tend the store."

I didn't believe for a minute that her father was getting

too old. What I did know was that Peggy hated housework and that she wanted to run the store.

"I guess this is it." She held up an envelope and examined it. "It sure is a mess. The writing is pretty, though. It don't look like your pa's. I can hardly read what he writes."

Before she could open the account books to prove her point, I grabbed the envelope out of her hand, shoved it into my pocket, and almost ran out of the store.

I waited to get home before I pulled out the letter. I examined the envelope. Peggy was right; it was a mess. I wondered what in the world had happened. It was wrinkled and smelled of tobacco and fish, and in the folds and creases were brown stains. It had been sealed with a wax blob. The ink was blurred and smudged and hard to read. I could barely make out the name written on the front. I think it was *M. Malarkey*. I was sure Pa meant the letter for Malachi, but I wasn't doing anything wrong. My first name started with an *M* too.

I picked the wax blob off with my fingernail and opened the letter. Inside was a folded piece of paper and another envelope. I carefully unfolded the paper. The writing on the sheet was the same fancy writing as that on the envelope. I squinted. I moved the paper from side to side and then up and down, but I couldn't make out the words. I finally went back outside where the light was better. I slowly read: *Dear sir, I am writing this for your* ink stain. *He says you are to come out.* The next three lines were missing because the paper had been folded and then gotten wet. There was just a hole left.

Matt married a singer. See Barney smudge *San Francisco.* Where there should have been a signature was a long brown ink line.

I opened the smaller envelope and pulled out a cleaner sheet of paper. When I first looked at it, I thought it was nothing but a bunch of lines and arrows. But then I realized it was a map of sorts, only there weren't names on it, just little drawings. I studied it for a few minutes more. The little wavy lines, I decided, could be a river and the two little boxes, houses. That might mean a town. Up in one corner was a star, and in another corner was a big circle. What they meant, I had no idea.

I turned the paper around to see if there was anything else. Pa had sent us what looked like a map, and he had gotten someone else to write a letter telling Malachi to come to California. I squinted at the letter again. It didn't exactly say "Malachi," though, it said "you." *California.* I let the word sort of stay on my tongue for a moment. I wondered if the word *America* had sounded as exciting to Grandma when she was in Ireland.

I looked back at the cabin. Except for Mama's grave, there was nothing that tied me to this place. This is my chance, I said to myself. If I don't do it now, I might never get out.

It was almost midnight when Malachi got home, but I waited up. "We heard from Pa, and he wants us to come to California," I said before he even had the door opened properly.

Malachi stared at me. In the candlelight it was difficult to see his expression. Then he let out a whoop. "Jehosaphat!" he shouted. "I'm going to Califorony! I'm going to be rich!"

"We're going," I corrected.

"Did Pa say that?" Malachi asked.

"He knows you couldn't go by yourself," I said.

"He said he would send for me. He said girls couldn't go to California. I heard him," Malachi argued.

"And how will you get there? What are you going to use for money?" I asked.

For a minute Malachi looked confused. "We could sell Ben or the chickens," he finally said. "And maybe some of the furniture." He casually laid his hand on Ma's rocker.

"I'll thank you to take your hands off that," I said. "Ma said that rocker and the quilt were mine."

"Well, shoot, if'n you don't let me sell something, what am I supposed to do?" Malachi complained.

"Face it, Malky, you can't hardly read your name." I shoved the letter under his nose. "Read what this says."

Malachi peered at the paper for a minute and then pushed it away. "I can ask people where them places are."

"And have every thief and his brother finding Pa's gold? You need me. You'll be wandering all over California looking for Pa."

Malachi looked at the letter again, and then he frowned. "You just told me that we wouldn't have enough money to send me. Where we gonna get money for two? Besides, I never heard of no girl going to Califorony."

I took the letter with the map back again. I could just imagine Malachi gambling it away. "Now you have," I said.

Convincing Malachi that I was going with him turned out to be the easiest part of getting to California. The biggest problem was that I didn't even know exactly where California was, much less how to get there.

All that night I kept wondering how we could find our way out west, and then I thought of Mrs. Throckmorton. Maybe she would know how her husband had gone. Their farm was about two miles from ours. The next morning I hitched up old Ben to the wagon and drove over to her house.

When I arrived, a dozen cats came from the barn and started winding themselves around my ankles.

"Scat, scat," Mrs. Throckmorton said to the cats as she followed them out of the barn. Mrs. Throckmorton was nothing like her husband, who was tall and skinny. She was a plump little woman with fluttery hands and a high-pitched giggle.

"Bless me, is this Molly? I never realized what a pretty young lady you've become. Come in, come in. I have fresh bread and tea or apple cider. Just leave the horse there and come on to the kitchen. I'd suggest the front porch, but the wind this time of day blows up something fierce."

I brushed the dust off my shoes. I noticed that Malachi's old boots were getting holes in the toes. They had never fit me very well, but I didn't know where I could get another pair. Pa always said that if I could get my foot into the boot, that was good enough, and he wasn't wasting money on buying something I didn't need. Malachi had gotten so much bigger than me that even when I stuffed the toes of his old shoes with paper, I walked out of them. But I had to have shoes, and it didn't look right to go visiting barefoot.

Mrs. Throckmorton bustled around the kitchen. "I'll get the kettle to boiling. Come, come, sit down, dear. No point standing if you can sit, I always say. Now then, tell me, have you heard from your brother and father?"

"Well, in a way," I said slowly. "But it was hard to read what he was saying. Have you heard from Mr. Throckmorton?"

Mrs. Throckmorton giggled. "Oh, I don't expect to hear from him." She patted my knee. "Dear, Mr. Throckmorton and I have separated. Oh, I hope I haven't shocked you? But you see, he really wasn't very nice. He gambled and drank, and he would smoke those dreadful cigars in my parlor. And it is *my* parlor. This was all my daddy's." She waved her hand around to include, I suppose, the whole farm. "My husband didn't have a penny to his name, and I'm afraid he didn't take to farming. I much prefer having a hired man who usually knows what he's doing. So when this gold nonsense came up and he wanted the money to go, I told him if he would just go and not ever come back, I'd give him the money. And he agreed, and so"—she laughed again—"here I am and, my dear, it is so nice not having that dreadful man messing up my house."

Well, I thought, would wonders never cease!

"Now, my dear, here I've just been chattering away. Can I help you in any way? Not that I'm not delighted if you just came to visit."

"I wondered if you knew how they went?" I asked.

"Of course I know how he and your pa got to California!" she said. "I wasn't going to let that man have my money and then one day find him back on the doorstep and hear he'd never gone anywhere! Now first of all, I realized it would be much faster for them to go by sea. Here we are, not that far from the Atlantic Ocean. I mean, it would be just plain foolish to have to go to that city—St. Louis, I think it's called—and then travel all those deserts and mountains by wagon train. I hear the trip is just dreadful, and if one meets up with Indians, why, heaven knows what could happen! No, that didn't make much sense. It doesn't pay to be penny-wise and pound-foolish, I always say. If you're aiming to get out there before anyone knows about it, then you must go by ship, I told him. I even went to Boston with them and made sure they bought the tickets. You know how childish men can be. Just like them to gamble the money away before they ever would get on board. Mercy, I'm not that stupid."

I suddenly realized that even though Mrs. Throckmorton looked like a silly woman without a thought in her head, under that mess of curls and ribbons and bits of lace, there was a very smart lady.

"No," I said.

"So, have they found gold yet, or did your father want money to come home?"

"I think they found some. Or he wouldn't want Malachi to go out there. But we don't know how to go."

"Surely you aren't thinking of going too?"

"I need to keep an eye on Malachi," I explained.

"Oh, I think you're making a mistake," she said. "I'm sure California is just full of dirty, nasty men. You wouldn't like any of them. If you have nowhere to go, you can stay here with me. What fun we could have! I always wanted a daughter. Don't go, dear."

"I'll be fine," I said. "But I need to find out how to go and how much it costs, if you don't mind telling me, that is."

"It wasn't cheap," Mrs. Throckmorton said. "Of course, the easiest way is on a sailing ship that goes around Cape Horn, but that takes the longest time. There is another way. When we got to Boston, I found that they could take a mail packet down the coast to a place called Chagres in Panama, and then they could cross over by river part of the way to Panama City and get a ship there to San Francisco. I had to pay four hundred dollars for Mr. Throckmorton to get that far. Maybe the cost has gone up, since more people must have heard about the gold."

"But where would Pa get money like that?" I asked. "I know he took one of our horses and some food supplies, but I don't think any of that was worth four hundred dollars. Besides, he had Matt along. That would be eight hundred dollars."

"Maybe he stole it," Mrs. Throckmorton said. "I'm sure you know he wasn't the most honest of men."

"But who would he steal from?" I said. "I haven't heard of anybody being robbed."

Mrs. Throckmorton shook her head. "I don't know. I gave Mr. Throckmorton some spending money. I certainly couldn't have him begging in the street; after all, he is still my husband, in name at least. Maybe he gave your father some of that," she said. "But now to the matter at hand. Are you bound and determined to go? There's nothing I can say to discourage you?"

I shook my head.

Mrs. Throckmorton stood up and shook out her skirt. "Then, my dear, I'll make a deal with you."

"A deal?" I asked.

"Yes. Now, I'm much too old to be traipsing all over the country, but I have to admit looking for gold sounds very exciting, and a good way to make money. Suppose I stake—I think that's the word—you. I'll pay for your and Malachi's way out there, and any gold you find, why, half will be mine. Does that sound fair?"

I looked at Mrs. Throckmorton's round, rosy face. I wasn't sure if her idea was fair or not, but what could I do? I had to trust her. "All right," I said. "But I can't speak for Malachi. I don't know if he'd want to share."

"Oh, never mind Malachi. I don't expect he'll find much. No, it's you I'm depending on. If you agree, I'll have my solicitor write something out," she said. "Not that I don't think you're honest, but I just think everything should be all neat and tied up, don't you? Come by in a few days, and I'll have the money for you."

I hoped I was right in trusting her, but there was no other way Malachi and I could get to California.

"Now then, when you get to Boston, go straight to the wharf. You can hire a mail packet there that's going down the coast. Of course, other ships may do the same thing. I suspect the best thing to do is ask around. Remember, you need to go to Chagres," Mrs. Throckmorton said.

I nodded, silently repeating the information to myself.

I stood up. "Thank you very much. I promise I'll send you your share of any gold I find."

"Of course you will, dear. Now, what will happen to your farm?" she asked.

"Pa didn't say anything," I said. "He owes Mr. Hawkins a lot of money, so I thought I could give the chickens and the cow to him in payment. We'll need the horse and wagon to get to Boston. I imagine I will just lock up the house and go."

"If I'm passing, I'll check up on it while you're gone," Mrs. Throckmorton promised.

Malachi never questioned where I got the money. I told him I had made a deal with Mrs. Throckmorton, and he accepted that. I think if I told him I had found it on the road, he would have accepted that too. It was obvious that Malachi needed me.

3

I locked the cabin door for the last time. It was now early October, and the air was cold and smelled of fall: dead leaves and woodsmoke. Malachi sat in the wagon blowing on his fingertips. I was surprised that I felt a little sad; not too sad, just a little. Although I had cleared off Ma's grave and said goodbye, shutting that door seemed so final. I suddenly realized that I probably would never be back.

All the preserves, the chickens, and the fresh produce that was still growing, I gave to Mr. Hawkins. I gave the rocker to Mrs. Throckmorton. We were leaving with our few clothes and enough food to last us to Boston.

"Come on. The house isn't going anywhere."

"You're right." I had gathered my clothes into Grandma's quilt, and now I threw it into the back of the wagon. I climbed up beside Malachi. He shook the reins, and as we started off, I looked back. We had never been on a trip before, and now, not only were we leaving our town, we were leaving the state. I felt as if I were leaving Margaret Mary Malarkey too.

In a way the trip was disappointing. An adventure should be exciting and different, but all we passed through were small villages and fallow fields.

We slept in the wagon and cooked our food along the way. By the time we got to Boston, we looked like vagrants. My skirt was streaked with the soot and ash from our cookfires. My hair hadn't been properly combed since we'd left home. Malachi didn't look any better. He had burnt a hole in the sleeve of his shirt, and he needed a shave.

Before Ma had married Pa, she had worked as a housemaid in Boston. Her stories made me think that Boston was some magical place filled with fancy people dressed in rustling clothes made of lace and shiny satin who lived in big houses with green grass and stone statues of animals in front. Ma had talked about the big church she used to go to with the rest of the servants and how it had colored windows. She said it felt peaceful, sitting there with sunlight shining through the stained glass turning all of them purple, red, and gold. I think Ma missed going to Mass after she got married and left Boston, but there weren't services in our town. Sometimes a priest would come through to baptize, marry, or bury people.

Even if we had had a church, I don't think Pa would have gone. He always said that he'd leave God alone and

God could leave him alone unless God wanted something, in which case Pa said he'd try to oblige, although he couldn't rightly see where God could want anything of Murray Malarkey.

Now as our wagon rattled across the cobblestones, I didn't think Boston looked magical. All I could see were dark, grimy brick houses all smashed together. They looked as though they would fall down if they had to stand by themselves. The city smelled of fish and rotting greens and too many people.

"Phew, it stinks!" Malachi complained.

"Ma would be horrified," I said. "We look like two beggars."

"Now that we're here, what do we do?" Malachi asked.

"I guess we need to find a place to stay and then find a ship captain who's going to Chagres." It had sounded easy enough when I first had made my plans, but now I wasn't sure. Boston was big and scary.

I remembered Ma used to say that rich people could afford a view, but poor people had to live where the work was, so we started looking for a room near the wharf. The wharf was simple enough to find since the masts of the sailing ships were clearly visible. We drove around until we saw a ROOM FOR RENT sign in a window.

Malachi stopped the wagon, and we climbed down. The front door was set into a windowless wall of brick. Malachi hammered with the knocker. The door opened a crack, and a wrinkled face topped by a white mobcap peered out.

"What do you want?"

"Have you a room for rent?" I asked.

"Aye. That's what the sign says."

"My brother and I would like to see it."

"Would you, now?" The woman came out and looked us up and down. She nodded her head. "Seems like you've been on the road for a spell. I'm Mrs. Needham," she said. "Come in, it's only a room, no place to cook. I find roomers would like as not burn the place down—and no visitors, either. Brother and sister, eh? Well, as luck would have it, there are two beds; room's not very big, you understand, but I trust it'll do. I keep a clean house, mind, no carousing or parties, but then you two don't look like you know any of them bad sorts, wharf rats I call them. Come in, now, don't be standing with the door open letting out all the warmth." She paused for a breath, and Malachi and I stepped into a small hall with four doors opening onto it and steep stairs leading up into blackness.

She ducked into one of the doors and came back carrying a lighted oil lamp. "I should never have bought a row house. Hardly any windows at all," she said. "It's like living in the depths of hell." She gathered up her skirts and, in spite of looking so old, bounded up the stairs.

I had thought our cabin was a poor excuse for a house, but when I looked around that room she was showing us, I decided that maybe Pa had done better for us than I realized.

"Nothing wrong with it," Malachi said, ignoring or

probably not seeing the spotted bedcovers and the small streaked window.

Mrs. Needham lingered in the doorway. "You be looking for work?"

"No," Malachi said. "We're going to Californy."

She nodded. "Heard about gold being there. I thought maybe it was just so much talk."

"I saw some," Malachi said. "It was right on our kitchen table."

"Well then, there you are. Now, if you want information about ships, you should see Cap'n Waltham. My late husband, God rest his soul"—she made the sign of the cross—"was a seaman out of Salem with Cap'n Waltham, before the big clippers brought the business to Boston. Had a dear little house in Salem. Mr. Needham never liked them big clippers. 'Great ugly brutes,' he used to say, 'practically need a town of sailors to sail 'em.' I always thought they were pretty with all them white sails."

When she paused for breath, I quickly asked, "Where can we find this Captain Waltham?"

"Pig 'n' Saddle Tavern. Two blocks over, down near the docks. Sailors are there all the time. But things don't get lively until it's dark. I don't recommend you going there though, miss. Your brother surely could." She smiled, revealing several blackened teeth. "Here now," she said, fishing around in her pocket and handing me a key. "Mind, don't lose it, or"—she looked at Malachi—"don't be lending it around. Here I am chattering away, don't have many young ladies staying here. I get hungry for a bit of women talk, I do. When your brother goes over to the Pig 'n' Saddle, you just pop in and we'll have a spot of tea. Down the stairs, last door on the right."

"She talks too much," Malachi said when Mrs. Needham left.

"She's just lonely," I said. "And now at least we know who to see."

Malachi shrugged. "Some old sailor who ain't sailed in fifty years, I bet. If I have to go to that tavern, I'll need some money, you know."

I dug out four bits from my pocket and gave it to him. I looked around the room. There was a basin on the washstand but no water in it.

"You better get some water and clean up first," I suggested.

"I don't need to wash," he said, rubbing his hands down his pant legs. "You can get water from that old busybody when I'm gone."

"Find a place to stable Ben before you go to the Pig 'n' Saddle," I said.

He nodded. "Don't know how late I'll be." He was whistling as he went out the door.

I took the pitcher from the washstand and went downstairs. Mrs. Needham had two snug rooms at the back of the house that were so crowded with furniture, it was hard to move. It looked as if she had stuffed everything from her "little" Salem house into them.

"Never mind the clutter, love," she said. "Here now"—
she pushed a cat off a rocker—"sit down. So, off to California, are you? Not many woman are headed out that way,
leastways not nice girls like you. Planning to make a fortune? Used to be money was made in whaling. People never
seem to be able to find treasures in their own hometown. Too
easy, I suppose. Just your brother and you? No folks?" She
actually stopped talking and waited for an answer.

"Our pa's out there already," I explained.

"Mr. Needham and I never had children. It was lonely
when he was out to sea. Salem was full of sea widows,
though. It made for company."

"Did you know my grandmother, Mary Margaret Winthrop?"

Mrs. Needham thought for a minute. "Seems like that
name is familiar. Did she have a little house near the harbor?
Least that's what I recollect. And she had a little girl."

"That was my ma!"

"Was it, dear? Will wonders never cease? As I always
said, it's a small world."

It was a comfort talking to Mrs. Needham, although she
talked more than she listened. She stuffed me with tea and
hard crackers out of a tin. Before I started up the stairs carrying not one but two pitchers of hot water, she gave me a
quick hug and told me to come see her anytime.

I couldn't sleep. I was anxious to hear what Malachi had
found out. It was almost dawn when he finally came in.

"Where have you been!" I said, sitting up in bed. "Did you find that captain? Is there a ship leaving?"

"Can't I get some sleep first?"

"No," I replied. "Look at me. What are you hiding?"

"I got a ticket," he said.

"A ticket?"

"You can't go," he said. "There's no point in crying and carrying on like a female neither. I told you it was a dumb idea, you coming along. I knew it wouldn't work. Now you're stuck here in Boston, and what are you going to do?"

"And why can't I go?" I asked.

"Because only men are going out there, that's why. They're not selling tickets one at a time. The men are forming something they call a company, and you buy a piece of the company and then the whole company hires a ship, or part of the ship. Leastways that's how it was explained to me. It was pretty confusing. But I found one of them companies, only they said all the tickets or whatever they call them were sold and there wasn't room for no more, but . . ."

"But what?" I said.

"Well, we started to play cards, and one of them ran out of money, and he bet his ticket and he lost and I won."

"Why didn't you keep gambling and get another ticket?" I said.

"I couldn't do that. It's like a club, they're all men. Don't you understand? No girls are in the club."

"You didn't have to tell them I was a girl," I said. "You could pretend I was a boy."

"But you're not," Malachi said.

I decided I wasn't going to argue with him, but I refused to believe I had gotten to Boston only to have to go back to the farm. There must be a way, I muttered to myself.

Malachi threw himself down on the bed, and before I could think of anything else to say, he was snoring.

I stepped over Malachi's jacket, picked up my shawl, and went outside. Wisps of fog were drifting down the street softening all the grimy houses, making them look gray and almost clean. It was early. Only a few men with tin lunch-pails and a woman or two were walking along the street. I could get a job on the ship, I thought. I could cook—with all those men, somebody would have to cook. Or if there was a cook already, I could do the washing up. Men didn't like to wash up.

The fog seemed to be thickening, and for a while I became confused as to where the wharf was. But finally I could make out the silhouettes of masts, floating eerily in a sea of vapor. I found the wharf as busy as our town was on market day at home. Men driving wagons steered their horses around the barrels and sacks piled on the wharf. Shadowy figures scurried up and down the gangplanks unloading or loading the almost invisible ships. I picked my way around the barrels and ignored a man who grabbed at the corner of my shawl.

"Hey, missy, what you looking for?" the man asked.

"Leave her alone, can't you see she's only a kid?" His friend turned to me. "Do you want something?"

"I'm looking for the ship that's taking the men partway to California," I said.

"California, is it?" He looked down the wharf and spit some tobacco out of the corner of his mouth. I pulled my skirt back away from the odious stream of amber liquid. "These here are whalers, miss. What's the name of the ship?"

I shook my head. "All I know is that it's due to sail in a few days."

The first man winked at me. "Fellow run away?"

"Don't pay no attention to him, miss. Down at the far end there're some smaller ships, mail packets, steamers, and such. I heard some packets might be taking men heading for California. Here, Billy, look smart. Take the lady down and show her where the mail packets are."

Billy was a skinny kid with a wide, friendly smile. He put down a crate and tucked a ragged shirt into a pair of pants so large that he had tied them up with a piece of rope. He touched the bill of his dirty cap and grinned at me. "Sure thing."

"I think I can find it myself," I said, but Billy had already started down the wharf.

"Don't say nothing," Billy said after I caught up to him. We had gone far enough down the wharf so the men couldn't hear us. "I'd a heap rather be just walking than stacking. What ship you looking for?"

"One of those ships that are going down the coast," I said.

Billy nodded. "I heard about them. They stop at some

Spanish town. Sailors say you have to hike through jungles and swamps and over mountains afore you get another boat for California, though. Really think there's gold there? Papy says it's just so much talk by folks who don't want to work. I'd go if Mr. Clyde would let me. Be a cabin boy, see all them places with savages and strange animals. Someday when I'm bigger, I'm going to run away and be a sailor."

"I know there's gold in California," I said. "I've seen it right on my kitchen table. And I'm going out there and get some for myself. My brother gambled for a ticket on the ship and got lucky, but I figured I could work for my passage, cooking or cleaning or something."

Billy stopped. "You can't do that. Girls aren't allowed on ships. Sailors think it's unlucky."

I stared at him. We were about the same size, so I could look him right in the eye. "You're crazy. My grandmother came from Ireland on a ship, and she was a girl."

"Oh, they can ride on ships, but they can't work. I tell you, it's bad luck."

"Why is it bad luck?" I asked.

"I don't know, sailors are superstitious, and I'm saying they won't let you."

He looked so smug standing there grinning at me like a monkey, I felt like smacking him. 'Course it wasn't his fault, but he didn't have to look as if he agreed with that silly tradition.

"So," Billy said, "you won't be going to California, but don't feel bad. I bet your brother will bring you back some gold. I heard it makes real pretty jewelry." He turned and looked along the wharf. "Hey, I got to go. Mr. Clyde will think I'm a sluggard." He started to walk away and then turned. "I think the packet is the *Meridee*, but it won't do you any good."

I nodded. I didn't want to walk past all those men again so I just kept walking and thinking. I was sure Billy was right that I couldn't get a job, but that didn't mean I was giving up.

4

I stopped when I got to the *Meridee*. It didn't look like the big whalers with their white sails. The *Meridee* was smaller, with a large wheel at one end and a smokestack in the middle. What Billy had said weighed on my mind.

"Something I can do for you, miss?" a sailor called to me from the deck.

"No," I said. "Thank you."

This part of the wharf was almost deserted. The *Meridee* was the last ship, and then the wharf ended. Around one of the big sheds that were filled with barrels and crates, I saw a narrow walkway. At the other end was a street with the same dark, smashed-together buildings as on Mrs. Needham's street, but here, instead of dark doorways, there were a number of shops on the ground floors. The sun had started to break through, shredding the fog and warming the cobblestones. One of the shopkeepers was dragging old furniture and baskets out to the sidewalk.

"Morning, miss." He touched his cap.

I nodded and almost went past when I noticed through the open door clothes piled on a front counter. I suddenly realized that if Billy could work on a ship, then why couldn't I pretend to be a boy and do the same thing? All I needed would be the right clothes. I turned to the man. "Do you carry clothes for children?"

"Why yes, miss. What do you need?"

I took a deep breath. "Well, you see, I have this younger brother, he's thirteen and he's going to California with my older brother who lives here in Boston, only this younger brother, he's just come here and my ma's been sick, so you see, since he's grown so much this last year, why, he don't have enough clothes. Ma said she never saw anybody grow so much in a year, you could almost see him sprouting up, just like a weed."

I paused. I couldn't believe I had spun such a yarn, but I remembered one of the bigger boys at home always telling fanciful tales at school when he hadn't done his homework. "Talk enough, and people stop listening. Pretty soon all they want is for you to shut your mouth," he had said to me.

I decided he was right. The shopkeeper wasn't even looking at me now. When I had stopped talking, he merely said, "What size is he?"

"I don't rightly know, but he's as tall as I am and I guess he's about as big." I was about to start going on about my brother being just a runt who suddenly began shooting up, but before I could open my mouth the storekeeper had disappeared into the back room.

In a minute he came out with a pile of clothes. He picked up a pair of dark pants and squinted at me. He put them down and dug out another pair and held them up.

"This should do," he said. "How many do you want?"

I thought quickly. I wouldn't have to pretend to be a boy forever. No sense spending any more money than I had to. "One pair and a shirt," I said. "And a cap."

"What supplies do you want?" he said.

"Supplies?"

"You said your brothers were going to California. They'll need prospecting tools. Axes and shovels. Most of the gentlemen are bringing pickaxes and chisels and such. And tin plates and cups and a kettle. Do they have blankets or bedrolls? They'll need a trunk too. And I have a gem of a machine in the back that's guaranteed to separate gold from rock."

I stared at the man. Buying all that stuff would take all the rest of our money. Besides, shopkeepers always try to bamboozle people to buy things they don't need.

"I'll tell my brother what you said."

While the man was ringing up my order, I held up the pants. They looked like they should fit. I wasn't sure about the shirt, but I could hardly try it on right then. I laid them back on the counter.

"Now, you be sure to tell your brother about those supplies," the man said as he wrapped the clothes. "I can't promise there'll be any left if he doesn't buy them right away. I hear ships are starting to leave for the goldfields."

I nodded my head and took the package. The sky was bright blue now, but a cold, stiff wind was blowing off the water. I hugged my shawl tighter around me. When I left that morning, I had memorized the way from the boarding-house to the wharf and so it was easy to retrace my steps. Mrs. Needham must have heard me come in, because before I was all the way up the stairs, the door to her rooms opened and she popped her head out.

"Your brother went out a while ago, luv. If you get lonesome later on, you come right on down. I always have tea water simmering."

I leaned over the banister. "We're expecting our younger brother," I said. "Could you leave the door unlatched for just a bit until he comes?"

I was glad Malachi had gone out, although I hoped he wasn't playing cards. Knowing him, he was likely to lose the ticket he had. I pulled off my dress and petticoat. My undergarments were plain so I wouldn't have to worry about lace or ribbons showing. I unwrapped the bundle and pulled out the pants.

They were too big around the waist, but I used the string from the package as a belt. When I buttoned the shirt, I found it was a little tight across my bosom, but it would have to do. I knew Malachi would never return them for me.

Besides, I didn't trust him in that store. That man would sell him things we didn't need and would be a burden to us.

The only mirror in the room was a cracked sliver of glass propped near the water pitcher. It was impossible to see all of me at the same time. I put the cap on and tried to shove my hair under it, but strands kept escaping. Maybe I should cut it, I thought. But then I didn't want to pretend to be a boy forever. Just long enough to get on the ship. I took off the cap in disgust. I hated my hair. It was orangey red and had a life of its own. It wouldn't stay neatly braided, and when I tried to fashion it into a bun, it kept escaping and hanging around my face. Ma had smooth, brown hair that I thought looked much more elegant.

I finally twisted my hair up and, holding it with one hand, managed to push it under the cap. Then I went downstairs and knocked at Mrs. Needham's door.

Mrs. Needham frowned at me when she opened the door. "Yes?"

I swallowed a laugh bubbling up. "I'm Molly Malarkey's younger brother," I said.

"Of course," Needham said. "Lord a mercy, you look just like your sister. Have you been up to their room yet? Molly's there, I saw her come in."

"She sent me down to meet you."

"Now that's sweet, come in, come in. Will you be going to California too? Although I do worry about Molly going. It just doesn't seem any place for a girl. Would you like some cookies? All boys are hungry—my nephews would eat me out of house and home."

"Mrs. Needham, it's me!" I pulled off the cap.

Mrs. Needham stepped back. "Molly? My Lord, child, why are you all dressed up like that?"

"You were right," I said. "I'd never get on board as a girl. So I decided I'd dress like a boy."

Mrs. Needham sat down in her rocker and fanned herself. "I don't know what to think."

I sat down facing her. "Malachi has a ticket, and I can't go back to the farm. And besides, there's Mrs. Throckmorton. I owe her money, and she's expecting me to find gold for her. And I want to go. It's not just the gold. I hate the farm. Ma never liked it either, and I know she'd want me to go. Going to California is like a wonderful adventure."

"Well, I'm sure I don't understand all this talk about adventure, but my husband—God rest his soul—he always had to be on the move."

"Do you think I can fool people?"

"People see what they think they should. And wearing those boys' clothes, why, they'll just assume that's what you are. If you're set on going, maybe it's best playing at being a boy. Safer. You can't be sure what kind of men you'll meet. No point my telling you, some of them aren't gentlemen, and I don't think that brother of yours would trouble himself to watch out for you."

"Malachi can't even watch out for himself," I said.

"I'm still not sure how wearing boys' clothes will get

you on that ship, though," Mrs. Needham said. "The way you tell it, there are no spaces left."

"I figure if he won a ticket for himself, he could win one for me," I said.

"Seems like you're dreaming, child, but I hope you're right."

When Malachi saw me in pants, he burst out laughing. "What a fool idea! Who do you think would take you for a boy in that getup?"

"Mrs. Needham didn't recognize me, and she said people would see what they expected to see, and if I'm dressed like a boy, then that's what they'll think."

"That old lady," Malachi said. "I bet she needs glasses. I think you're crazy. Even if you do fool people, you don't have a ticket."

I smiled sweetly at Malachi. "But you're so clever at cards. I know you can win another."

"No, sir," Malachi said. "The men aren't happy that I beat their friend. Some of them think I cheated."

"Did you, Malky?" I asked.

"I don't need to cheat. I'm good, but people think I'm stupid so they don't pay attention to what I'm doing."

"Well then, you should have no trouble winning again," I said.

"Why should I?"

"I have all the money," I said. "And I'm not giving you any more. So even if you have a space on that ship, it won't do you any good. You need money to eat and to play cards. So you have to do it."

Malachi rolled his eyes. "I don't want to, and I don't think that getup is going to do you any good."

Maybe Malachi was right. But I didn't have to fool anybody for very long. Once I was on the ship, there was nothing anyone would be able to do about it. Leastways, I didn't think so.

"I need money if I'm going to get you that ticket," Malachi said. He watched me go over to Grandma's quilt. I untied it and then opened the sack where I had put our money and counted out some coins, which I handed over. Malachi watched me put the money bag back into my quilt, but as soon as he pocketed the coins and left, I pulled out one of my petticoats and rolled it around the bag and put it back into the quilt. I doubted if Malachi would go through my undergarments.

Maybe I'm misjudging him, I thought, maybe I should trust him more. But then I decided I couldn't be too careful. We had no idea what might happen to us before we found Pa and the gold.

5

The next morning I went downstairs to see Mrs. Needham.
I found her easy to talk to.

"Come in, come in," she said. "Have you found a way
to go yet?"

I shook my head. "According to Malachi, none of the
men in the company were willing to risk their tickets in a
card game with him. I guess I have been foolish and silly to
think I could go just because I wanted to. Pa had always said
reading made people addlepated. Maybe he wasn't so
wrong after all."

"But you still want to go?" Mrs. Needham said.

I nodded. "I feel like just hiding somewhere on the
ship."

"Become a stowaway! Lass! Lass! Don't be foolish. I've
been thinking. If you're so set on going, maybe I can help, al-

though I want you to know it's against my better judgment. Tomorrow morning I'll pop over to the wharf and see what I can do. The ship is the *Meridee*?" she asked. "That's Cap'n Waltham's ship. Perhaps he would have room for a girl, although I'm not promising anything. But you need to make other plans if you can't go."

When I returned to the room, I found Malachi lying on the bed.

"I don't have a ticket for you," he said. "And I'm leaving in two days, so you better start making tracks home, less'n you're planning on staying here with the old lady."

"It's all right," I said. "Mrs. Needham is going to talk to the captain."

Malachi snorted. "What's she going to talk about? Does she think she can get you on the ship? It sounds like crazy talk to me."

"I don't know," I said.

"I wouldn't hold my breath," he said, but I noticed he looked a little worried. Maybe it had just occurred to him he might be on his own.

The next morning I saw Mrs. Needham leave the house and turn down the street that led to the waterfront. I whispered a little prayer. When I heard her return a few hours later, I ran down the stairs to meet her. She was smiling.

"Come along now," she said.

I followed her into the parlor.

"Well," she said, "I'm not sure you'll be that pleased

with the arrangements, but they're the best I could do. Men are fighting for a space on his ship. It's full to the gunwales."

"But am I going?" I asked. I couldn't imagine what arrangement would be so bad I would refuse.

Mrs. Needham wandered off to her small kitchen, placed the teakettle on its hook, and swung it over the fireplace.

"Do you know how to care for small children?" she asked, coming back into the parlor.

"Small children?" I said. "I thought the ship would be full of men going to California."

"Yes, of course, but it is a mail packet, and it does have a regular run to Chagres. There is a couple, Mr. and Mrs. Dorset, an American man and his wife, and two little girls who are going to Panama. The father is opening up a trading business there with a Panamanian. The person they hired to watch the girls has run off, and the mother is quite distraught and insists she can't put a foot on that dreadful boat, as she calls it, unless she has a baby nurse. Her personal maid refuses to become a nursemaid. Says it's beneath her. I don't think Cap'n Waltham was pleased hearing the *Meridee* called 'that dreadful boat.'"

"How old are the girls?" I asked. "I've never taken care of small children before. Do they understand that?"

"Now, how was I to know something like that?" Mrs. Needham protested. "I told the cap'n that you came from a large family, which is true."

"Yes, but I was the youngest," I explained. "What will I have to do?"

Mrs. Needham threw her hands up. "I'm sure I don't know, never being blessed with babes of my own. But you're a sensible girl. I'm sure you can manage."

There's no point fretting, I decided. After all, if Pa had let me stay in school, I would have become a schoolteacher and then I would have learned about children. Besides, with only one day left before we sailed, I didn't have time to worry about two little girls.

The next day Malachi and I took Ben and our wagon to a blacksmith that Mrs. Needham recommended and sold them both. I gave Ben a final apple and then watched him being led away. I suddenly felt scared. Ben was our last link to the farm. For a second the whole plan seemed crazy. But then I thought, no, this is my chance to do something exciting.

I took the money from the blacksmith and shoved it into my pocket.

"Don't I get any of that?" Malachi said. "I don't have anything in my pockets at all."

"Not now," I said. I was afraid if I gave him some money, he might start gambling and lose his ticket. Even I was not stupid enough to think I could go on the trip alone. And I would only be with the Dorsets until we got to Panama. Besides, I needed the money to buy a dress. I didn't think a nursemaid should be in a dress that was old, dirty, and too small. And I certainly couldn't wear the pants I had bought.

"Don't worry, luv," Mrs. Needham said when I asked her where old dresses were sold. "Let's see what I can find."

She took an oil lamp and a bunch of keys and told me to follow her up to the attic. "I used to be much smaller," she said. "Perhaps there's something you can use."

The attic smelled musty. Mrs. Needham put the lamp down and swiped her hand over the top of a trunk to remove the dust. Then she lifted the lid. The trunk was full of clothes. She picked up a dress with flowers printed all over it and shook it out. "Too fancy," she said, "the material would just tear." She dug deeper in the trunk and pulled out several more dresses. "It's too dark up here. Let's take them downstairs to see what we have."

"My," she said after we had returned to her parlor and spread several dresses out on the couch. "I had forgotten about some of these. When Cap'n Needham went on whaling trips, he would bring back bolts of material." She held up a plaid dress made out of a shiny material that rustled when she shook it out.

"Taffeta," she said. "It looks fancy, but it's a strong material. I'm not sure it will be very practical for what you need, though."

I stroked the skirt. I had never felt anything like it before.

Mrs. Needham looked at me. "Well, you never know when a good dress is needed," she said. "You take it." She picked out two other dresses that were made of serviceable cotton and one made of something she called linsey-woolsey.

"After dinner we'll see if we can do something with them," Mrs. Needham suggested.

That night Mrs. Needham fixed a special dinner of cod and boiled potatoes and brown bread. Malachi came, although I suspected it was only because he had no money and nowhere to go. He sat on the edge of his chair and replied to Mrs. Needham's questions with one-word answers. He didn't look very comfortable, and once supper was over, he slipped away upstairs. Mrs. Needham brought out her sewing basket. "Let's see if we can fix up these dresses. I'm afraid they're a bit out of date, but I don't fancy clothes will be important in California. Now then, you just slip this one on, and we'll see what needs to be done."

I unbuttoned my dress and let it drop around my ankles. When Mrs. Needham saw the condition of my undergarments she made a clucking sound.

"I don't know what I was thinking," she said, shaking her head. "I should have looked in that old trunk a day ago. Well, never mind." She handed me one dress, and I put it on.

It was too big around the waist and a little short, but I had never had such a pretty dress before. Mrs. Needham put on a pair of spectacles and peered at the hem. "I think there's enough material here to let down," she said. "And a belt around the waist should pull it in. Do you know how to sew?"

"Ma taught me," I said. "But all I ever did was mend the boys' shirts. I never had any pretty material like this to sew."

We sat in the glow of the oil lamp. I picked out the old hems, and Mrs. Needham neatly made new ones. It was after midnight when we finally finished.

"Now, you run off to bed," Mrs. Needham said. "I'll just give these dresses a once-over with my iron and leave them for you."

I hardly slept that night. I was scared and I hadn't expected to be. Suppose the mother didn't like me and then the captain threw me off? Malachi was snoring in the next bed as if he didn't have a care in the world, and I guess he didn't. After all, I had always looked after him, and as far as he knew, I still would.

The morning was cold and foggy. Outside the door on a chair Mrs. Needham had left the dresses, a belt, and two surprises; a petticoat trimmed with lace, and a straw bonnet. Malachi had slept in his clothes, so he just tied up his things in his old blanket and dragged them down the stairs. I put on one of the dresses and rolled the others up in my quilt. I decided I might as well bring the boys' clothes too since I wasn't sure what I would need in California. Then I put on the bonnet and wrapped my mother's shawl around me and thought to myself: If it wasn't for Malachi's old boots on my feet, I would almost look respectable.

When I went to say goodbye to Mrs. Needham, she agreed that I did indeed look respectable. "Don't worry, the family will be most impressed." She gave me a hug. "Now, you remember, if you ever need anything, why you just tell Cap'n Waltham, or when you get to California, you send me a letter."

I promised I would, and then Malachi and I set off. It

was still dark, and the wind felt icy against my cheeks like it was fixing to snow. The wharf was crowded with men. Most of them were loaded with suitcases, pans, axes, and whatnot. It looked as if that shopkeeper had talked quite a few into buying an awful lot of equipment. I even saw a large wooden machine that looked like it might be the one that was guaranteed to separate gold from rock.

When I started up the gangplank, the men stared at me. I was stopped at the top by a big man with a bushy beard. "Do you have a ticket?" he said, holding out his hand.

"No," I said. "I'm to see Captain Waltham."

"I have one," Malachi said, shoving his precious paper at the man.

"Fine," the man said, and gestured Malachi to go on board. Malachi nodded and I watched him disappear. I couldn't follow, and I knew he would probably find the gamblers and drinkers to hang around with, but at the moment there was nothing I could do.

The man frowned at me. "You'll have to step aside, you're in the way."

"I'll find the captain myself," I said and, without looking back, marched onto the ship. I hadn't gone a few feet when a sailor stopped me. "You're not allowed on board, miss, unless you have a ticket."

"Where is Captain Waltham?" I asked. "I have orders to see him."

The sailor looked as if he didn't believe me. "I'll see if I can find him, miss, but you have to step aside. You're in the way."

I moved over to a corner, and in a few minutes an older man appeared.

"So, you're the lass Nelly Needham told me about?"

I nodded.

"I hope you know what you're getting yourself into," he said. "The father, Mr. Dorset, seems nice enough, but his wife is a terrible woman. One of those who takes to her bed if she is the least bit inconvenienced."

I swallowed hard.

"Too late for her to find anyone else, though. Come along," he said.

The captain went down a short flight of stairs into a narrow corridor and knocked on one of the doors. I hung back. The door was flung open by a tall man. Ma would have said he was a proper gentleman, with his white shirt so clean it almost dazzled my eyes and a fancy neckpiece that disappeared into a vest made out of shiny material embroidered with flowers. I suspect Pa would have said he was putting on airs, trying to be better than hardworking folks. I had to admit, I was partial to Pa's version.

"Yes?"

"Begging your pardon, Mr. Dorset, but this is the lass I was telling you about, the nursemaid for the little ones." The captain pushed me forward.

"Who's there?" a voice from the room asked.

The man turned away, and I tried to see who was talking, but the room was too dark.

"It's the girl the captain found for us," he said.

"Well, bring her in and shut the door. You know the light is making my head throb."

The captain tipped his cap, backed out of the doorway, and disappeared. Mr. Dorset closed the door. The cabin was small, and everywhere I looked were boxes and trunks spilling clothes. I gaped at the mounds of lace and ribbon.

As my eyes got used to the gloom, I could see a lady lying on a narrow bed built into the wall. There were more of those wooden beds around the room. A woman in a black dress and white apron with a silly-looking bit of lace plopped on her head was picking up clothes from the floor and shaking them out. She gave me a smile and jerked her head. I glanced in that direction and saw two little girls sitting on trunks in a corner. One was sucking her thumb and the other was crying softly.

The woman on the bed raised herself on one elbow. "Don't stand there, come over so I can see you."

I moved across the cabin. She took the cloth from her forehead and said, "Nora, come and change this cloth. It's quite dry and doing me no good at all."

Nora dropped the dress she was folding and took the cloth.

"And this time use cold water to dampen it."

Nora bobbed her head and left. The little girl who had been crying softly now began to wail loudly.

"Mr. Dorset, please see if you can stop Harriet. My nerves can't take any more."

"Stop that immediately, Harriet. Don't you know your mama has a dreadful headache?" the father scolded.

Harriet hiccoughed loudly and went back to whimpering.

"Well, don't stand so far away," Mrs. Dorset told me. "And take off that odd bonnet, I want to see your face."

When I went closer, holding my bonnet, Mrs. Dorset looked me up and down. I was sure she noticed Malachi's old boots. She turned to Mr. Dorset. "Is this the best the captain could find?"

"We didn't give him much time, and he assured me an old friend recommended her."

"What's your name?"

"Molly Malarkey," I said.

"Irish." Mrs. Dorset sighed.

"Have you had any experience taking care of young children?" she asked me.

"I understand she comes from a large family," Mr. Dorset explained.

Mrs. Dorset leaned back against the pillows and groaned.

"Now really," Mr. Dorset said, "it's not for long, and what harm can the girls get into on board a ship? They can't run away."

I looked over at the little girls, who were staring at me. I smiled at them. The one with the thumb in her mouth took it out and smiled back. Harriet gave her a poke, which knocked the smaller one off the trunk. She immediately started to scream.

"Take them outside!" Mrs. Dorset demanded. "Mr. Dorset, find their coats and hats and have that wretched girl take them. Where is Nora? Doesn't she know how I'm suffering?"

Mr. Dorset sighed and started shuffling through a mound of clothes. "I don't know what is wrong with that maid. Can't she keep things in some kind of order?" he said, more to himself than to me.

"Maybe I can help," I said. "What colors are their coats?"

"I'm sure I don't know," Mr. Dorset said. He kicked a small trunk out of his way.

"Harriet," I said, "if you can find the coats and hats, I'll take you out to look at the ship. Maybe we'll see it leave the dock."

Harriet slid off the trunk and grabbed her sister's hand. "This is Edna. I'm five and she's three."

"Harriet, stop talking," Mr. Dorset said.

Harriet stuck out her lip and stomped her foot. "I don't like it here!" she screamed. "I want to go home!"

Edna looked at her sister, and her lip began to tremble. I quickly said, "Let me guess. Is this your coat?" I picked up the first piece of clothing I could find. It was a white lace petticoat. Harriet stopped screaming and started to giggle. "No, silly. All our things are over here." She pulled a small trunk from under one of the wall beds.

"My coat is red," Harriet explained, "and Edna's is blue."

I found the wraps and put them on the girls. When I started to button Harriet's, she pushed me away. "I can do it myself," she insisted.

It was a relief to get the girls out of that dark room. I steered them along the passageway toward the stairs. It was hard to walk; the ship seemed to be rocking back and forth. Edna kept bumping into the wall. I held on to her as best I could.

We met Nora as we started up the stairs. She was carrying a pan of water and winked at me as she passed.

When we came out on deck, the light was dazzling. I grabbed the girls' hands tightly. Harriet tugged on my hand and tried to pull away.

"If I were you, I would put a rope around them," someone next to me suggested.

I turned around. The young man who had spoken looked like he was laughing at us.

"You mean like a cow?" I said.

"More like a dog," the man replied. "Are these your sisters? Let me introduce myself. My name is Kevin Doyle."

I wasn't sure what to say. What was the proper thing to do? When Ma had talked about Boston and what it was like to live in a house working for wealthy people, she always said well-brought-up young ladies never talked to young men without being introduced properly. When she had told me that, it certainly didn't seem very practical information—

in our small village there weren't any strange men to talk to. But now, here was a strange man. How should I act?

Mr. Doyle reached down and took Edna's hand. "And what's your name?"

"Her name's Edna," Harriet said, "but we're not supposed to talk to strangers."

"But you know my name," he said. "And now I know your sister's name. So we're not really strangers anymore. Shall we shake hands?"

Harriet looked at me.

"Mr. Doyle," I said. "I am the nursemaid for these little girls, and I don't think their parents want them talking to people they don't know."

"Quite right," he said. "But it is a small ship, and we will all be in a foreign country soon, and I think it's nice if everyone could be friendly, you know, and help each other out."

He did look nice, not scary or mean. I took a deep breath. "My name is Molly Malarkey."

"Ah," he said, "and what are you doing on a ship heading for Chagres?"

"The same as you, I imagine," I said. "I'm going to California."

"Alone? Or are these little girls going to California too?"

I suddenly noticed he had taken Harriet's hand, which left me free to get a tighter hold of Edna.

"No, the girls are going to Panama with their parents, and my brother's on board."

"Your bodyguard?"

I laughed. "You could say that."

"Well, I'm off to California too," he said. "Before I settle down and help my uncle with his medical practice, I wanted to see something different. A gift to myself for finishing my training."

Doctors were respectable, I decided. And I was sure that if Dr. Doyle became too forward, I could always tell the captain. Edna started to pull at me. "I want to see the water," she said.

"Edna, you have to be very careful when you're on deck," Dr. Doyle said. "You don't want to get hurt or to fall overboard now, do you?"

"I don't like this place," Harriet complained. "We can't do anything. And it's windy and cold."

"It will soon be warm," Dr. Doyle said. "We're heading for the equator."

A sailor came over to us. "If I was you, miss, I'd take the little ones below. We're ready to leave, and they'd be in the way. We can't have them getting hurt."

I decided to take the sailor's advice. "Goodbye, Dr. Doyle," I said. "Thank you for helping me with the girls."

"It's been a pleasure talking to you. And please call me Kevin."

Now that's a proper gentleman, I said to myself. I was sure Ma would approve of him.

6

By the next morning Mr. Dorset, Harriet, and I were the only ones who weren't seasick. I was glad that Harriet was well because I had to sleep with her. Nora was with Edna. She lay curled in their bunk, moaning softly. Edna was sitting up, crying and saying her stomach hurt and that she was going to throw up again. Harriet whined that she was hungry and that the cabin smelled bad. I hurried to get both of us dressed.

Mrs. Dorset demanded to see the captain, as if he could stop the ship from rolling. "There must be a doctor on board," she said when the captain finally appeared.

"I'm sorry, ma'am, but this isn't exactly a pleasure boat," the captain said. "Usually the cook takes care of any medical problems the crew has."

"I know a doctor," I said without thinking. "Kevin Doyle."

Mr. Dorset looked at me. "How do you know any of the passengers?" he asked.

"He was helping me with the girls yesterday," I said.

Mrs. Dorset sat up and frowned at me. "How could you let a strange man talk to my girls!"

I started to protest that I hadn't done anything wrong, but the captain shook his head at me. "Why don't you run up and see if you can find your doctor?" he suggested.

"I'm hungry," Harriet whined. "I want something to eat."

"Absolutely not," Mrs. Dorset declared.

"I think it would do the little one good to get some fresh air and a bit of food," the captain said. "Come along, I'll see what the cook can rustle up."

Before either parent could object, I grabbed Harriet's coat and hat and my shawl.

"I only talked to Dr. Doyle," I explained to the captain as we went up the stairs. "Wasn't that the proper thing to do?"

"A girl alone can't be too friendly. You have to remember that some men aren't gentlemen and would take advantage of you."

I thought of Malachi's friends. "I know," I said. "But Dr. Doyle was very pleasant."

"Just be careful," he said.

I looked around the deck. I was surprised to see that it

was almost empty. I didn't see Dr. Doyle—or Malachi, either. "What happened to everybody?"

"Seasickness. The first days out, that's what happens to landlubbers."

"I'm a landlubber," I said, "and I'm not sick."

"You're fortunate," the captain said. "But I don't see your doctor. It might be he's sick."

When Harriet started to complain, the captain leaned down to her. "Come on, little lady. Let's find you some food."

In the galley the cook sat us at a table in the middle of the room. It was an odd-looking table with a rail all around the edges, but when he put two plates in front of us, I understood what the point of the rail was. With every roll of the ship, the plates scudded back and forth.

Harriet started to laugh. "The plates are dancing," she said.

I didn't know what little girls should be eating, but the food the cook put in front of us didn't look like it was meant for a five-year-old. The bread was so hard, I had to dip it into my coffee before either one of us could chew it. There were eggs that weren't very fresh, but Harriet didn't notice.

When we were finished eating, we went back on deck. More men had come up from below. I found Malachi leaning against the rail. He looked green.

"Malachi, are you all right?"

Malachi frowned. "Nobody told me ships rolled all over the place." He looked at me. "You seem fine. I guess you have a fancy cabin and everything."

"Not exactly, " I said. "Harriet here and her father and me are the only ones who aren't sick."

"Try sleeping with fifty seasick men," Malachi said, and then he leaned over the rail and threw up.

When he felt better, he staggered over to a coil of rope and sat down.

"And is this your doctor friend?"

I turned. Mr. Dorset was standing behind me.

Malachi looked at Mr. Dorset and then ran back to the railing.

"No," I said, "that's my brother."

Mr. Dorset took Harriet's hand. "And what is your brother doing on this ship?"

"I thought Captain Waltham told you," I said. "We're meeting our father in California, and Malachi had a ticket, so Captain Waltham heard you were looking for a nursemaid and he suggested me."

"I prefer that my daughters don't associate with these rough men," he said.

I sighed. "Should I take Harriet back to the cabin?"

"For the moment you can stay here," Mr. Dorset said, "but I don't want Harriet talking to anyone."

"Yes, sir."

"And if you see that doctor friend of yours, tell him we need him."

"There he is," Harriet said.

When I waved, Dr. Doyle smiled and came over.

"Dr. Doyle," I said, "this is Mr. Dorset."

"How do you do," Dr. Doyle said.

Mr. Dorset nodded. "My wife is quite ill. We would like you to look at her. Come along, Harriet." Mr. Dorset took his daughter's hand, and then he turned to me. "Since Nora is ill, I imagine you might be of assistance to Dr. Doyle."

I followed them below deck.

When Dr. Doyle saw the condition of the cabin, he raised his eyebrows. Edna had been sick again all over the bunk, and Nora, looking green, was trying to pull the sheets off the bed. Mrs. Dorset was moaning.

Dr. Doyle looked at me. "How do you feel?" he asked.

"Fine," I said.

He turned to Mr. Dorset. "Sir, why don't you take Harriet back out for fresh air? I'm sure Miss Malarkey will be of more help here."

Mr. Dorset looked annoyed. I suspected few people gave him orders, but he took Harriet's hand and left.

Mrs. Dorset was convinced she was dying. "You must do something," she said.

"In a few days, you'll be right as rain," Dr. Doyle assured her. "I'll see if the cook can make you some tea. You need to try and drink some liquid."

He told Nora to sit down and rest. Then he helped me clean up Edna. We left her sitting on one of the trunks. There was a small round window in the cabin that Dr. Doyle said was called a porthole. He pushed it open, and a clean, salt-smelling breeze blew in.

"I'll catch my death," Mrs. Dorset complained.

But Dr. Doyle convinced her that fresh air was the best thing for the three of them.

He got me some clean sheets from one of the sailors, and we remade Nora and Edna's bed. Edna climbed onto it and almost immediately fell asleep. Nora lay down next to her.

"They'll all be fine," he said. "Seasickness doesn't last very long, and the sea will soon be calmer since we're heading south."

He was right. In three days everyone except Mrs. Dorset seemed to be feeling better. I suspected Mrs. Dorset wasn't as sick as she made out. She struck me as one of those women who "enjoys poor health," as Ma used to say. The captain had set aside a part of the deck for the use of the Dorset family. He assured Mr. Dorset that his crew would keep the miners away. I guess Mr. Dorset had decided that Kevin—as he insisted I call him—was respectable enough because he allowed Kevin to visit our part of the deck.

The captain supplied us with chairs, and Nora found the girls' toys and books. The weather suddenly started to turn warm. It was like we were sailing away from winter. One day Mrs. Dorset agreed to come out on the deck for a while. Since she was there, she agreed I could take a break to find Malachi.

He was sitting on the deck, just staring off into space. He complained that he had lost the little money I had given him, and that some men seemed to be real cardsharps. He even suspected they were dishonest. And he was convinced that we should have bought all those supplies the other men had. He had heard that there were no supplies at all in California.

"That's silly. Surely Pa has all we need."

"Maybe so," Malachi said, but I could see he didn't believe me.

Suddenly one of the sailors let out a shout. "Flying fish on port bow!"

I gasped to see several huge shiny gray fish appear out of the water and leap into the air.

"I never heard of fish flying!" I said in amazement.

"Beautiful, ain't they, miss?" a nearby sailor said. "We're in Caribbean waters."

Caribbean, I whispered to myself. Even the word sounded exciting.

Just then some of the miners appeared from below deck with rifles in hand and started shooting. One of the fish jerked in midair and fell back into the water.

"Molly!" I heard Mrs. Dorset scream. "Come here and take the girls to the cabin immediately. Those men are nothing but animals!"

I ran back and grabbed the girls' hands. "What's that noise?" Harriet asked.

"It's just some of the miners behaving in a silly way," I explained. "Come on now, before your mama gets mad at you."

I could see the captain had come on deck and was demanding the miners turn over their guns.

"You can't do that," I heard one of the miners say.

"I can and I will. I am the captain of this ship, and my word is law."

I was certainly glad that Malachi didn't own a gun.

The captain came to our cabin later to apologize for his passengers' behavior. "I can assure you that the girls will be perfectly safe up there now."

I hoped Mrs. Dorset would agree. The weather had been getting warmer, and I couldn't imagine having to stay in the stuffy cabin for the rest of the voyage.

"Please, Mama," Harriet said. "It's hot down here, and I want to see those funny fish."

"I'm sure the captain has control of the situation," Mr. Dorset insisted. He was sitting on a trunk next to the porthole with an unopened book on his lap. "And Harriet is right. It's stifling here. I think it would do your head a world of good if you went back outside."

"I know I'll have nightmares about those men and their nasty guns," Mrs. Dorset said. "But if Molly promises to watch the girls very carefully, and if she keeps them away from everybody, including her brother, I guess they will be fine."

"Yes, ma'am," I said. I really couldn't blame her for being angry at the miners.

By the eighth day it was getting harder to keep the girls entertained. They soon grew tired of watching fish, and I had read all of their books to them so often we knew them by heart. Kevin helped by telling them stories, and some of the sailors even showed them how to tie knots and make a "cat's cradle" with string.

"How many more days before we get to Panama?" I asked Kevin.

"We get to Chagres in two days. And then we have to cross the Isthmus to get to Panama City. Have you and your brother any plans to get from there to San Francisco?"

I shook my head. Everything seemed so complicated. I had thought that once I left Boston, there would be no more problems. I guess I wasn't as smart as I assumed. Maybe I should have questioned Mrs. Throckmorton more.

Kevin must have seen how I felt. "Probably Malachi's company has made arrangements." He tried to sound hopeful.

"But that would only be for him. What have you done?" I said.

"I have a ticket for the steamer that's supposed to stop at Panama City. But I've heard rumors that the ships aren't very reliable, so maybe you're no worse off than I am."

The next day Nora and I started to reorganize the Dorsets' luggage. Mrs. Dorset claimed she couldn't stand all the mess and noise we were making, so she consented to spend more time on deck. How I longed to be free of her.

7

In the late afternoon, fourteen days after we left Boston, we arrived at Chagres. The night before, Nora and I had finished repacking all the Dorsets' belongings. The Dorsets dined with the captain.

"I hate this," Nora said, looking around the tiny, sweltering cabin.

"What?" I asked.

"Boats and terrible food and waiting on women like Mrs. Dorset. My mother said being a lady's maid was a proper job and, if I was clever, I could meet a nice butler or valet and live a genteel life. I want to marry Jacob Essex and be a farmer's wife, but my mother hates farms and thinks I should hate them too." Nora sat down on a trunk. "Maybe I should have gone to work in the mills. Anyway, I'm going back. They can't make me live in some foreign place not knowing a word people are saying to me and listening to Mrs. Dorset complain."

"You're staying on the ship? Can you do that?"

"They can't make me get off," Nora said. "Besides, I asked the captain, and he said it was between the Dorsets and me. Why don't you come back too, Molly?"

"No," I said.

When I went on deck the next morning, every spare inch was covered with the miners' gear. They were busy hauling up even more equipment from the hold. I didn't see Malachi, but I was sure he was around. I saw the Dorsets' luggage piled near the railing.

Our ship had anchored a couple of miles out in the bay. I leaned over the railing and stared in astonishment at the water. It was filled with small boats that looked like logs. In them were dark, small natives waving and yelling at the ship.

Mrs. Dorset came on deck. "Molly!" she said. "Get away from the railing at once. Mr. Dorset says those men are naked!"

"Not really," I said. "Just on top." But I obliged her by pulling back.

"What are they saying?" I asked the captain.

"They're offering the passengers rides to shore."

"Why do we need rides to the shore? Where is the gang-plank?" Mrs. Dorset asked.

"Our ship can't come any closer," the captain said. "The bay is too shallow."

"How will I get off?" Mrs. Dorset said. "I can't swim! And I'm not getting into a boat with half-naked savages!"

"They are not savages, and I would warn you to treat them with courtesy," Captain Waltham cautioned. "You'll be lowered in the lifeboat."

"That little thing? It will tip over, I just know it will."

"It's very steady, ma'am. And my sailors will be very careful. You will be perfectly safe."

Mrs. Dorset turned to Mr. Dorset. "I want to go home."

"Don't be foolish," Mr. Dorset said.

"If you're ready," the captain said, "I'd advise you to start for shore. I understand it can be difficult to hire natives to take you up the river. There are only so many guides and many miners."

"Up the river!" Mrs. Dorset repeated. "We have to go on another ship?"

"Not a ship exactly," Captain Waltham said. "More like a large canoe. I think it's called a *bungo*."

At that news I thought Mrs. Dorset was going to have a conniption.

"Stop screaming," Mr. Dorset said sharply. "You are scaring the children." He picked Mrs. Dorset up and almost dumped her into the lifeboat. "Come along, Harriet," he said. "Get in. Molly, take Edna's arm. Where's Nora?"

I didn't say anything. I hadn't had a chance to talk to Nora, but I noticed she had hidden a box off in the corner of the cabin. Probably her clothes.

"What about my luggage?" Mrs. Dorset asked.

"It will be lowered in nets into a bungo," the captain said.

"I don't understand what has happened to Nora," Mr. Dorset said. "Where is she?"

Captain Waltham looked embarrassed. "I'll search for her, but we will have to shove off soon. We have a schedule to keep."

As the boat started down, Mrs. Dorset clung to the side, her eyes shut tight. The lifeboat rocked as it descended, occasionally banging against the side of the ship. I thought it was exciting. We landed with a splash, and water sprayed over us.

"My bonnet!" Mrs. Dorset said. "It's ruined!"

As we sat on the water bobbing next to the ship, I looked up and watched the sailors push a net filled with our luggage over the side and lower it into a bungo. I noticed Nora leaning on the railing looking down at us.

"Goodbye!" she called. "I'm going back home. I've decided I don't like being a lady's maid, and I miss my family and Jacob. I hope you find gold, Molly."

"But you're my maid," a shocked Mrs. Dorset called up to her.

"Not anymore," Nora said. She waved at us and disappeared from the railing.

"She can't leave. Mr. Dorset, say something."

"There's nothing we can do," Mr. Dorset said as a sailor pushed the boat away from the ship and he and his companion started rowing toward the shore. "If she doesn't want to come, we can't make her. I'm sure we can find another maid in Panama City, and meanwhile we have Molly."

Mrs. Dorset dismissed me with a glance. "I need someone to manage my clothes," she said.

"I don't think your clothes will be a problem right now," Mr. Dorset said. "And Molly has been very dependable. She will work out fine."

"But I'm not staying in Panama—I'm going to California," I objected.

"Impossible," Mrs. Dorset said. "That's not at all proper for a young girl!"

Being proper wasn't the most important thing to me. And I didn't agree with Mrs. Dorset's idea of what was proper anyway.

When the boat landed on the beach, we were immediately surrounded by natives who were chattering at us as if we understood their language. They grabbed our luggage out of the bungo that had followed us.

"Here! Here!" Mr. Dorset said, trying to wrestle one of his bags back. "You can't steal our things."

"They're not stealing, sir," one of the sailors said. "They want you to hire them to ferry you up the river."

"Are they to be trusted?" Mr. Dorset asked.

"Of course, if you treat them fairly," the sailor said. "And I'd advise you to hire them immediately before some of the other passengers do. If you want my help, I'll be glad to oblige. A few of them speak English, and I speak a little Spanish."

Once the native who had Mr. Dorset's bag saw that the sailor was going to help, the guide gestured to a few of his friends to take the rest of the baggage out of the boat. Mr. Dorset followed the sailor and the first native up the beach, picking his way around the other passengers with their bags and tin dishes and tools—all the stuff the storekeeper in Boston had tried to get me to buy—and the Indians who were busy trying to hire out their boats.

I looked around to see if I could find Malachi. I felt a little guilty not keeping better track of him, but on the ship there hadn't been much I could have done for him. My job had given me no free time, and besides, I couldn't exactly go into the hold where Malachi was. After watching the behavior of the miners on deck, I could only imagine the swearing and drinking that went on belowdecks. Finally I spotted Malachi with some of his friends. They were arguing with a group of natives in loud voices and waving their arms. I doubted if they were treating the natives with courtesy.

One of our sailors helped Mrs. Dorset out of the boat. Harriet scrambled after her. I lifted Edna up, and the sailor put her on the beach. As if by magic, native women appeared from the crowd, followed by children. They stared at Mrs. Dorset. One even touched her skirt. Mrs. Dorset frowned and pulled her dress away. Another woman untied Edna's bonnet. Edna's eyes grew round, but she didn't cry. Harriet reached out to one of the children and ran her hand down the child's thick black hair. The girl giggled and started to feel Harriet's blond curls, and then she ran away.

"Put your bonnet back on," Mrs. Dorset said.

Harriet ignored her and started running after the little girl. The village women laughed and tried to lead Edna away.

Mrs. Dorset looked totally bewildered. "Mr. Dorset, come back here!" she called in a frightened voice.

"They are just being friendly, ma'am," the sailor said. "I'm sure your girls are perfectly safe. Why don't you just relax and wait until your husband comes back?"

"I'll go after Edna and Harriet," I said.

"I should hope so," Mrs. Dorset said. "That is your job, after all."

Chagres was like nothing I had ever seen. I was used to a farm with more rocks than hard soil and a little green that we slaved over in order to keep our vegetables growing. Here, everything seemed bathed in green. And there were strange noises. Something was howling and chattering in the trees. Birds with bright feathers kept screeching and flying from one branch to another. I found myself turning in circles trying to see everything.

Dogs were all over the place. Some looked like the mutts we had at home that roamed around and stole food—yellowish dogs with long thin faces and mean-looking eyes. But there were other small hairless dogs that barked loudly when anyone approached them.

I found Edna and Harriet sitting in a hut made of stalks and leaves. The women were squatting around them in a circle, laughing and smiling. Edna and Harriet looked a little scared. When they saw me, they got up and one grabbed my hands. I smiled and nodded my head at the women and tried to show them I was friendly but that I was taking the girls.

I pointed back toward the beach and said, "Mama."

"*Sí, sí,*" one woman said, but when I started to walk away, all the women gathered around me.

The women didn't look angry, but I didn't know exactly what they wanted me to do.

I pointed again toward the beach. "Mama," I repeated.

"Having trouble?"

I turned and was relieved to see Kevin. "I don't know," I said.

The women gathered around Kevin, chattering.

"Slow down," Kevin said, but I didn't think anyone understood him. Then he said something to them in what sounded like their language.

"I didn't know you spoke Spanish," I said.

"Some of the sailors taught me a little on the trip," he said. "I think the women want you to eat with them. Maybe it's their way of welcoming you."

"I don't think their mother would like the girls eating different food," I said.

"I'm sure you're right," Kevin said. He hoisted Edna up on his shoulder, took Harriet by the hand, shook his head at the women, and began walking away. I ran after him before the women tried to make me stay.

I'm not sure what I expected Chagres would be like. I

thought there would be a place where people could buy food and sleep. But the town had nothing but huts made out of what looked like big leaves. Kevin told me he had learned the roofs were made of cabbage leaves. They didn't look like any cabbage leaves I had ever seen. The sides of the houses were bamboo stakes.

"What will we do for food?" I asked Kevin as we walked along the beach.

"Most of the men will probably pay the natives for food. I can't imagine the Dorsets doing that, though. Perhaps Captain Waltham will give them some of his supplies. Don't worry, we won't starve."

I was sure we wouldn't. I took Harriet's other hand. If Pa and Matt could get to California, then I certainly could, even if it meant eating very strange food. Knowing Pa's temper, I wondered how many guides he had angered or cheated. And I could see that Malachi's group was behaving in a boorish way. I wouldn't blame the residents if they were hostile to us.

Thankfully, the captain did send us enough food to last until we got to Panama. I think he was afraid Mrs. Dorset would refuse to leave and he would have her on the return voyage. Kevin said the natives would provide places to sleep and supply food for money, but Mrs. Dorset refused even to go into one of the huts. After much weeping, she finally agreed to sleep in one of the bungoes.

Unlike the boats that had circled the ship, these had little shelters made of leaves and grass over part of the boat.

Our boat was big enough to hold all of the Dorsets, myself, and their trunks if we were sitting up, but it certainly wasn't big enough for all of us to sleep in. With Mrs. Dorset stretched out in the front of the boat and the girls bedded down in the rear, there was little room for Mr. Dorset and myself to be comfortable for the night.

"I'll be all right on the beach," I said.

Some of the miners who could not find a hut to sleep in had lit fires there and were preparing to camp out for the night. Malachi came over to talk to me.

"Where are your friends?" I asked.

"Sleeping in a hut," he said. "But they thought somebody should keep an eye on the boat we rented, and I lost the toss. I need more money. We have to pay these people to take us to some place called Gorgona, and then we have to rent burros. And I'll need money to live in Panama."

I nodded. I was surprised he hadn't been asking for more money all along. "I'll give it to you in the morning."

Once he left, I pulled out my quilt and found the money pouch and untied it. I counted out some coins for Malachi, then buried the pouch in my bundle of clothes.

Mr. Dorset was off by himself. I had seen Kevin nearby, talking to some of the guides. After a few minutes he came over and sat beside me. For a while we quietly watched the flickering lights of the bonfires. I was surprised how warm it still was. Suddenly I found myself twitching. There was a strange stinging sensation along my legs. I leaped up, shaking out my skirt.

"Something's biting me!"

Out of the corner of my eye I could see Kevin scratching his ankle.

"Fleas," he said.

"Fleas?" I lifted my skirt, not too high of course, and saw little black specks jumping on my legs.

"Ugh! This is disgusting! They're all over the place."

"They're probably worse in the huts." Kevin kicked at the sand. "Come on, we'll try sitting on the rocks."

I thought Mr. Dorset would follow us, but he sat stubbornly right where he was. He wasn't even scratching.

As we moved away from the beach, I noticed some miners coming back from the village. Some were tearing off their shirts, and others were dancing around as if moving would shake off the insects.

"I hope they didn't pay much for sleeping in those huts," I said.

The beach, already crowded, was now filling with more miners trying to find a bug-free place to lie down. I pointed to a particularly large piece of machinery that belonged to one of the miners.

"What is that big thing good for?" I asked. "How are they going to get it on those little boats?"

Kevin shrugged. "They have all these crazy machines that are supposed to get gold out of the riverbeds. Waste of money if you ask me. I think that thing is what they call a rocker. It sits in the river, and you put the gravel from the river into the top, and then you use water to wash out the gravel. The gold is heavier than the gravel, so that's supposed to be left behind. I asked some of the miners, and they told me that most of the rockers are much smaller than this one, about the size of a baby cradle. I guess the owner thinks he can mine faster with that contraption, but I'll bet it won't even work."

"A man in Boston tried to sell us something like that," I said. "Did you bring any equipment?"

"No," Kevin said. "I'm not convinced there's all that much gold out there."

"Then why are you going?" I asked in surprise.

"My uncle's a doctor and he paid for my training. He expects me to go to work for him and one day take over his practice. And I guess I'll do it, but Farmingdale is an awfully small town. I'm not ready to settle down and become a country doctor, at least not right away."

"So," I said, "you're really looking for an adventure?"

"Why not? And you? Are you expecting to get rich?"

"It would be nice," I said. "But that's not what's important to me. I just wanted to get off that farm. I was sick of being an unpaid maid to my family."

"Well, you're a maid now, aren't you?" Kevin said.

"Yes, but now I'm being paid, and besides, it's not forever."

Kevin nodded.

It was a long, uncomfortable night, and at the first hint of morning, the beach was a beehive of activity. Everybody was anxious to get going. The miners were ready, but none of the native guides who owned the bungoes were around. The men yelled a lot and a few shot their guns into the air, but the village stayed quiet. At last a group of miners went to the village and dragged several natives back to the beach. Other guides followed. The miners then stood over the natives while they loaded the boats with the gear. The biggest piece of machinery needed a bungo of its own. I watched the miner who owned it arguing with a native. Finally the red-faced miner handed over more coins.

Malachi came over to collect the money I had promised him.

"Why are you all being so mean to the guides?" I asked.

Malachi shrugged. "Hard to tell what they're talking about."

"Well, that's no reason for how you are behaving."

As Malachi started to leave, I called after him: "And don't gamble all that money away."

After a lot more shouting and arguing, most of the boats were loaded. I was glad that the Dorsets had made room for Kevin in their boat. He was good company, and he also seemed to be able to talk to the three boatmen. It was like having a nice big brother instead of the selfish clods I had been stuck with.

It took a while to arrange the bungo to Mrs. Dorset's satisfaction. She didn't want to sit in the bottom—she felt it would be undignified. Finally, Kevin and Mr. Dorset made a sort of cushion out of large leaves and arranged it under an awning. Mrs. Dorset accepted that. Mr. Dorset and Kevin sat at the front of the boat along with a native who had a large pole that he used to push the boat along. I was in the middle beside the luggage. Harriet and Edna sat behind me, so they were under the awning. The two other guides in the rear started to row. The bungo moved away from the muddy shore. All the other bungoes had left already, so we had the river to ourselves.

I could feel the swift current grab the boat and pull it into the center of the river. The water was as murky and green as the trees that leaned over the river. I could reach up and pull off some of the bright red flowers that grew on their branches. It almost seemed as if we were riding through a dark tunnel. The air was hot and heavy, and there was the constant buzz of flying insects.

But I didn't care. This, I said to myself, is adventure.

8

After an hour or two in the crowded bungo, I longed to stretch my legs. Although Mrs. Dorset never mentioned fleas, I noticed she would scratch herself when she didn't think anyone was looking. In the heavy air insects kept swarming around our heads.

At first the girls were quiet, watching the strange things that were on the shore. There were chattering monkeys that leaped from vine to vine, bright-colored parrots, and huge flowers. But when it rained, which it seemed to do every five minutes, the leaves of the trees dripped water all over us.

Mrs. Dorset kept fanning herself and sighing, but she seemed impressed by the flowers.

"Well, I never," she said. "The flowers are so big they almost look artificial."

Kevin reached up, picked one off, and handed it to Mrs. Dorset. As he did, he gave me a wink.

Mrs. Dorset smiled at him. It was the first time I could remember her smiling.

"Why thank you, Dr. Doyle," she said. "How nice."

The Indian next to Mr. Dorset muttered something and then laughed.

"I think he says the flower will die very quickly," Kevin explained.

"Well, it's pretty anyway," Mrs. Dorset replied.

Flowers didn't interest the girls for long. They began to get restless and complain of the heat. Edna started to bounce up and down.

"You have to be still," Kevin said, "unless you want the boat to tip over, and then we'll all fall into the river."

"I'm sitting still," Harriet said. She was trailing her fingers in the fast-moving water. "I don't know how to swim. Would I drown, Papa? What would you do if I fell in?"

"Don't even say such a thing," Mrs. Dorset cried. "My goodness, now my heart is beating like crazy. Oh, I know I'm going to get sick. Can't the men do something, the boat keeps rocking so!"

Mr. Dorset frowned at Harriet. "Now, see what you've done, upsetting your mother like that. Really, Molly, can't you keep the children quiet?" He turned to Kevin. "Perhaps we can go a little slower?"

I felt like saying that it wasn't as if I could take them out to play, but Kevin explained.

"I think it will be difficult to convince the boatmen to decrease their speed. They're anxious to get to Gorgona and turn around to collect another fee from new arrivals in Chagres." He dug into his pocket and pulled out some string. "Here," he said to Harriet. "You can make some cat's cradles. Remember what the sailors taught you?"

Harriet was quiet for a while, but Edna soon began to whine. I pulled her close to me and started to sing softly. Ma used to sing old Irish songs and sea chanteys that Grandma had taught her.

"I remember my good mother singing those," Kevin said. "Do you know this one?" He started to sing a funny song that made Harriet laugh.

"I want to sit next to Kevin," Edna said. She started to crawl along the bottom of the boat to get near him.

"Edna! Sit down and be still," her father said. But his warning came too late. Edna had bumped into one of the boatmen's paddles, which dropped into the river. He tried to grab it by leaning over the side of the boat, but the current was carrying it away from him. The boat started to rock.

"Stop that," Mr. Dorset shouted at Harriet, who was trying to stand up to see what was happening.

I grabbed Harriet's skirt to pull her back down, but before I knew what had happened, I found myself in the river choking on the water I had swallowed. I was still holding on to Harriet's skirts. She was thrashing around in the river, letting out little squeals.

"My baby's drowning!" I heard Mrs. Dorset scream.

I wasn't much of a swimmer. There was a small stream in our town, and in the spring when the snow melted, it almost became a river. The water would pool up near a bend in the stream and make a swimming hole. A lot of the boys of the town would go there, but they always swam naked. So when Lucy and I went swimming, we had to be sure the boys wouldn't be there. We would strip to our drawers and waists and splash around. I had learned to dog-paddle—not very well, but I could stay afloat.

I wasn't used to swimming in a deep river with a swift current, and it was hard to paddle and try to hang on to Harriet at the same time. She had her arm around my neck and was kicking me with her feet. I could feel her fingers in my hair. For a moment I was afraid we were going to drown.

One of the boatmen jumped into the water and swam over, grabbing me around the waist.

He shouted something in Spanish. I didn't understand his words, but by his gestures I guessed he wanted me to give him Harriet. Paddling with one hand, I managed to pry Harriet away from me. The boatman took her and handed her to another guide who had joined him in the river.

Mr. Dorset leaned over the side of the bungo and grasped Harriet under the arms, dragging her into the boat. He steadied the bungo while I dragged myself and my dripping skirts and water-filled boots on board. The boatmen climbed in after me. They shook themselves off, laughing between themselves as if our dunking was funny. I realized how foolish we must look to them with our layers of heavy clothing and piles of luggage in a place that was incredibly hot and rainy. Mr. Dorset made his way carefully to the back of the boat. The two men seemed surprised, but then they broke out in broad smiles when he pressed some money into their hands, and they immediately went back to work, using a spare paddle to replace the one that had been lost.

Harriet tried to crawl into her mother's lap. "You're getting me all wet," Mrs. Dorset objected as she shooed her off. "Molly, change her clothes before she catches a fever."

I looked at the pile of boxes and trunks tied together in the middle of the boat. I wasn't even sure I could find the girls' clothes. Besides, with the rain Harriet would be wet again in a few minutes.

"She'll be fine," Mr. Dorset said. "In this heat I don't see how she could catch anything."

"I don't understand why we can't go ashore for a while. I feel like I've been sitting forever," Mrs. Dorset complained. "And I would like her to have clean clothes; she smells of the river."

The river did smell—moldy and stale, the way vegetables do when they go bad.

Mr. Dorset sighed. "There isn't anywhere to pull the boat up."

In most places the banks of the river rose steeply. They were covered with tangles of trees and bushes. Sometimes there would be a break in the trees, and I could see a round hut or two with a cow or goat in front or a mangy dog that would start barking.

If we stopped now as Mrs. Dorset wanted, she would have to climb the bank. I suddenly had a picture of Mrs. Dorset with her many petticoats and soft leather boots trying to scramble up the muddy side. I grinned at the thought.

Occasionally we saw a small beach where Mr. Dorset suggested we stop, but the Indians ignored both him and Kevin.

"I suspect they have a favorite place," Kevin said. "After all, they know the river."

Mrs. Dorset sighed and fanned herself with a palm leaf. "I never dreamed it would be like this," she said. "It's like a terrible nightmare. I thought we could just sail to Panama City, and then you could go to your office and I would have a beautiful house and help with the children. I now wonder what our new home will be like. Surely we won't be living in huts?"

In a way I felt sorry for her. She didn't look like the same woman I had met weeks ago. Her dress was dirty and torn, and her hair, which Nora used to work so hard to make look just right, hung in wet tangles from under her soggy bonnet. The girls looked as if they had been playing in mud puddles.

"Panama is a city," Mr. Dorset said, "and my partner Mr. Sanchez has promised that he will find suitable housing for us. You just need to be patient. Really, you've been very brave, and it's almost over."

The sun was beginning to set when the Indians pulled the bungo into a small clearing where a few other bungoes had moored, but we didn't see any of the miners. Off in the distance we could hear yelling and swearing.

Once the bungo was secured, the boatmen wandered away. Kevin built a fire and we gathered around it. The flames seemed to discourage the mosquitoes and other flying insects. Mr. Dorset passed around some of the food Captain Waltham had given us, and we boiled water from the river, although none of us drank much of it. Mrs. Dorset and the girls slept in the bungo, while Kevin, Mr. Dorset, and I huddled around the fire. In the middle of the night I heard the occupants of the other bungoes returning, but I was too tired to care who they were or what they had been doing. Or if my brother was among them.

Mr. Dorset had said the trip was almost over, but that wasn't really true. The next afternoon we reached the town of Gorgona. There the river became too shallow for the bungo. We weren't in Panama but at a village that looked almost exactly like Chagres, except here there wasn't a bay. We were still twenty-one miles from Panama. According to Kevin, who had gotten the information from the natives, we would have to ride burros to get there because the trail ahead was narrow and rocky.

We dragged ourselves out of the bungo, and Mrs. Dorset collapsed on the beach. "I shall never move again," she said.

"Wait until she sees the burros," Kevin whispered to me.

Our boatmen unloaded the luggage and put it down in the first empty spot they could find. The small beach was already crowded with the luggage of the miners who had been with us in Chagres. Higher up on the beach, many of them had put up tents. Beyond the tents was the village, where, from the sound of shouting and laughing, many of the men had gone.

"Molly," Mrs. Dorset ordered, "find fresh clothes for the girls and myself. I can't stand the smell of these a second longer."

"Yes, ma'am," I said. I stared at our pile of luggage.

Kevin had found a group of men with a tent who were willing to let Mrs. Dorset and the children use it to change their clothes. I found the trunks that held their things, and Kevin helped me drag them to the tent. The only water we had was from the river, but with a damp cloth at least I could get some mud off the girls. When they were cleaned and changed, Mrs. Dorset demanded my attention.

"You'll have to help me unlace the back," Mrs. Dorset said. "Honestly, this is so tiresome! I cannot understand whatever got into that Nora to make her run off like that."

As I struggled with Mrs. Dorset's buttons and lacing, I wondered where Nora was. It seemed like months since I had last seen her, but it had only been a few days.

When Mrs. Dorset was finally dressed in fresh clothes, I started to gather up her old ones.

"Just throw them away. I can't stand the sight of them,"

she said. "I shall never wear them again. They smell of the wretched river."

Well, I certainly wasn't going to throw away perfectly good clothes, so I said nothing and covered them with my quilt. I pulled off my wet dress and petticoat and looked through my bundle to find something to wear. Then I discovered the pants and thought about the burros we would be riding. When I was little, I used to love riding our horse Ben. At first it didn't matter that my undergarments showed, but as I got older, even Pa had told me to start acting like a girl and stop making a public spectacle of myself. I must have looked a sight because usually Pa never cared what people thought. After that I only rode Ben when others, particularly boys, weren't around to see my bare legs and the edges of my pantaloons showing.

But if I was going to ride a burro, there was no way boys or men wouldn't see my legs. Maybe now was the time to wear the pants and shirt I had bought. When I was dressed, I was surprised how wonderfully free I felt, even though the shirt was too heavy for the hot, sticky weather. But there were no skirts flapping around my ankles and getting in the way, and the pants were looser around my waist than my dress had ever been. I fastened the belt around my waist and looked down at myself and had to giggle. What would Mrs. Dorset say? It didn't take long for me to find out.

"Molly, where did you get those clothes? You look positively indecent! What are you thinking of? Mr. Dorset, don't let the girls see her! Go and change immediately."

Mr. Dorset nearly smiled. "I think Molly is being quite sensible," he said.

"Mr. Dorset, I can't believe you said that." Mrs. Dorset started fanning herself. "You will never see myself or our daughters wearing such unladylike apparel."

"Why do you look like a boy?" Harriet asked me, which just got her mother more upset.

"You see! Even a baby realizes Molly looks most inappropriate."

Before Mrs. Dorset could make more of a fuss, one of the miners whose tent we had used came over.

"Begging your pardon," he said, "but my mates and I would be obliged if you would continue to use our tent for the night. It would be most uncomfortable for a lady and the little ones to sleep on the beach. But I must warn you that we plan to start at the crack of dawn, so you must be prepared to be up early."

While Mr. Dorset was busy thanking the men, Kevin started to gather up the rest of the Dorsets' luggage. I took Harriet and Edna and went to look for Malachi. I was beginning to worry about him.

I found him sitting alone on the beach.

"Where are your friends?" I asked, sitting down beside him and pulling Edna on my lap. Harriet squatted beside me.

"Thrown out," he said.

"Thrown out? What do you mean? What did you do?"

"Nothing," he said. "They've been after me since I won the ticket from their friend. They kept accusing me of cheating at cards. They said I'm out of the company and that I can just find my own way to California."

"Did you cheat?" I said.

At first Malachi didn't answer. He shrugged his shoulders and looked away. Then he said, "Now how will I get to Panama? It costs money to hire them donkeys or whatever they are. Those men took away all the money I won. They said if I complained, they'd have me arrested."

"I'll see what I can do," I said.

Malachi looked at me. "How much money do you have?"

"Enough," I said. "Not enough to have you playing cards and gambling, but I'll pay for your burro."

Malachi smiled. "I didn't like those guys anyway. They treated me like I was a stupid little kid."

I suspected Malachi was hiding something, but I had no intention of talking to the men in the company. Instead I went to Mr. Dorset and explained that my brother had had a falling out with his group and I was willing to pay to rent his burro, if he could continue on to Panama with us.

Mr. Dorset refused to take my money. "You've been a good girl and a real help," he said. "As long as your brother behaves himself, he's welcome to travel with us."

I reported back to Malachi.

"No gambling, no swearing, no drinking," I warned him.

"I don't swear," he said.

The tent was hot, but it was nice to be away from the flying bugs and the constant drip of the rain. It was also good to stretch out to sleep. Of course, there were still the fleas, but I had gotten so used to itching and scratching through the night, I didn't pay much attention. Although the tent was large, Malachi and Kevin slept outside because Mrs. Dorset said it wasn't proper to have a single young man sleeping in the same tent as her little girls.

It was still dark when I woke up the next morning. I could hear burros braying and men swearing. I dressed myself and crawled out from under the tent flap. Burros were tied together and standing patiently while men strapped boxes and valises onto their backs. Kevin, Malachi, and Mr. Dorset came around the corner of the tent leading seven animals.

"Take your pick," Kevin said.

Before I could choose which burro I liked, Harriet darted out of the tent. When she saw the burros, she ran to them, her hands outstretched.

"No! No!" Her father grabbed her. "They might bite you. They're not tame like your pony at home."

They looked tame to me. I reached out and stroked the nose of the nearest one and made soft crooning noises the way I used to do with Ben. "What a nice boy," I said.

"I don't think he understands English," Kevin said.

"He knows I like him."

With Malachi helping, Kevin and Mr. Dorset quickly loaded two of the burros with most of the Dorsets' luggage. The extra boxes and bundles were tied behind the saddles of the burros Kevin and Malachi would be riding. The poor animals stared at me with large, sad eyes. They didn't seem big enough to carry such heavy loads.

When Mrs. Dorset finally appeared, Kevin and Malachi quickly took down the tent, and Kevin returned it to the miners.

"Glad to help," the miners said.

Mrs. Dorset seemed confused when she saw all the burros. "You don't expect me to get on one of those filthy animals, do you?" She looked around. "Besides, I need a sidesaddle. The girls and I shall just have to walk."

"Ask the men if she could walk," Mr. Dorset said to Kevin.

Kevin shrugged, and then he turned and said a few words in Spanish to one of the natives who were leading the burro trains. The native shook his head before answering Kevin.

"He says the trail is hard and the lady would get hurt," Kevin told us.

"Can't we hurry up?" Malachi complained. "Half the men are leaving. If there are any ships at Panama, they'll be gone before we get there."

"Mrs. Dorset," her husband said, "there's no help for it.

Come along." He picked her up and placed her on one of the burros. She let out a scream and clutched at her skirts, trying to cover her lace-up boots and stockings.

"I can't ride like this," she said. "I'm a lady!" She managed to scramble off.

"Look," said Kevin, "why don't we try to build up one side of the saddle with blankets? Make it into a kind of sidesaddle."

It took Kevin and Malachi and Mr. Dorset almost an hour before they had arranged the saddle so that Mrs. Dorset was satisfied and Mr. Dorset thought his wife would be safe. To be doubly sure, Mr. Dorset tied her on. She didn't look very comfortable, but at least she was mounted and very little of her legs was visible.

Mr. Dorset put Harriet in front of him, and I had Edna in front of me. I could see that Mrs. Dorset wasn't happy that I was riding astride, but she said nothing. I think she began to realize that no one was noticing her, or me, either.

The sun was high in the sky when we started out. I had thought the trail would be a wide road or that at least the ground would be smooth, but what we seemed to be riding in was a narrow, rocky ditch. In some places the sides of the trail were almost head high and there was barely room for one burro to walk at a time. In other spots one side of the trail would just disappear over the side of a cliff so that our burros would have to hug the bank on the other side. Every so often a burro would lose its footing and slip sideways. Then rocks and pebbles tumbled down the edge, making a loud noise. The burros didn't seem to pay much attention. They would quickly regain their footing and continue on the trail.

Whenever our burro stumbled, it felt as if Edna and I were going to be thrown headfirst into the air and be pitched forward and trampled under its hooves. I clung to Edna so hard she finally started to complain.

"You hurt me!" she said. "Stop squeezing."

Eventually Edna fell asleep leaning heavily against me. I could relax a little bit and look around. I felt as if we were on top of the world. A mist rose from the valley below, but we were so high that it didn't reach us. And it was hot. Sweat gathered at my neck and spread down my back. My thick shirt clung to me.

When I got off my burro for a lunch break, I thought I would fall down. My legs felt like rubber. I had forgotten how long it had been since I had ridden Ben.

Malachi burst out laughing when he saw me leaning against a tree.

In spite of my aching legs, I stomped off.

Malachi followed. "Can't you make these people move any faster? Everybody must be in Panama by now."

"I don't think anyone can go twenty-one miles in half a day," I said.

I knew we were traveling slowly, but then the Dorsets were in no hurry. They didn't have to worry about catching a ship. By late afternoon we were far behind the rest of the miners. We had lost more time at lunch because Mrs. Dorset had demanded a long break to "pull herself together." And after a few more hours, when we reached a wide place in the trail, Mrs. Dorset insisted she couldn't ride another foot.

When Kevin explained to our guides that we wanted to stop there for the night, they got very angry. But after a lot of shouting the natives walked away, leaving us to unload the donkeys.

"We're stopping here?" Malachi said. "There are hours and hours of daylight left. None of the other groups are stopping."

"It gets dark very suddenly," Kevin replied. "Losing a day won't make that big a difference. And this is a good spot. We're off the trail, and there's a stream so we will have water."

Malachi grumbled as he started to unpack his burro. When he was finished, he went off by himself. The rest of us sat around the campfire. Almost all of the food Captain Waltham had given us was gone. We were reduced to eating hardtack dipped into boiled water. Harriet made faces as she crunched on hers. Edna refused to eat anything. She had a sip of water, and then she cuddled against me, sobbing.

"Tomorrow will be better," Mr. Dorset promised.

But of course, that wasn't true.

9

The next day was worse. The girls were cranky, tearful, and hungry. Edna didn't even want to get on the burro, and she wouldn't sit quietly once her father put her in front of me. By now there were few miners on the trail. Our guides were angry because we were going so slowly. After we passed some of the other guides leading their burro trains back, they began pushing and beating at their burros with the sticks they carried.

Harriet started to cry when she saw the men hitting the burros. Mr. Dorset stopped his burro and got off.

"Sit quietly," he said to Harriet.

He walked over to one of the natives. "There will be no more beating of the animals," he ordered.

The guide smiled and shook his head.

Mr. Dorset grabbed the stick out of the guide's hand. "No!" he said, waving the stick in the surprised man's face.

The man started muttering, and a few others raised their sticks as if to hit Mr. Dorset.

"Offer them more money," Kevin said.

"That's bribery," Mr. Dorset replied.

"Give them anything they want," Mrs. Dorset said. "Remember our girls."

Mr. Dorset handed the stick to Kevin and reached into his coat pocket. He showed the men several bills, and then he pointed to the stick Kevin still held. "No!" he said again.

One of the guides nodded his head, smiled, and put out his hand for the money.

"Only give him half now," Kevin said. He got off his mount and went over to Mr. Dorset. Kevin said something to the guides, and after a lot of head shaking and gesturing, the guide accepted the one bill Mr. Dorset offered.

"What did you tell them?" Mr. Dorset said.

"I told them they would get the rest when we arrived."

They both got back on their burros, and we started moving forward.

When we stopped for a rest, I asked Kevin how long before we'd get to Panama.

He shook his head. "If we push hard, we can probably be in the city tonight, but I don't think that will happen. Tomorrow for sure."

Malachi had been complaining all day. He was always riding ahead of us. I suspected he was hoping to catch up with a faster-moving burro train, but I guess he couldn't find any, because he kept rejoining us. Now he came over to sit next to Kevin and me.

"Suppose those ships have left when we get there, or there's no more room on them? Those guys cheated me. All of them have tickets to San Francisco but me. How are we going to get to California?"

"There'll be other ships," Kevin said. "And unless you want to risk traveling in the dark alone, I'm afraid you don't have any choice."

I knew Malachi didn't like to travel alone, so I wasn't surprised that he stayed. He just continued to whine as we struggled along.

In spite of the money, the guides kept trying to get us to move faster. While they didn't use sticks, they kept pushing and yelling at the animals. Finally a few of the burros broke into a trot, which scared the riders and made all the luggage tip dangerously to one side.

When Kevin pointed out a good place to stop for the night, the guides shouted at us and tried to keep the burros moving along. But Mr. Dorset reined in his animal and dismounted. Then he stopped the burro Mrs. Dorset was riding, untied her, and helped her down.

With much muttering, the guides halted the rest of the train.

"It's still light!" Malachi complained.

"We'll be in Panama tomorrow," Kevin said.

It was around noon the next day when we got our first sight of Panama City and the Pacific Ocean. The road had widened by this time and was even paved with big stones. The bay and the towers of what looked like a church sparkled in the sunlight.

"Only a few miles now," Kevin said.

"Let me down," Mrs. Dorset suddenly ordered.

"But we're not there yet," Mr. Dorset said.

"I don't care, I'm not arriving in Panama dirty and riding a silly donkey."

Not only did Mrs. Dorset insist on walking, but she first demanded I find a change of clothes for her and the girls. This meant Mr. Dorset had to unload her trunk from the burro's back.

Picking through their luggage, I chose three outfits. Mrs. Dorset found some bushes to hide behind. I shook out her dress and helped her change out of her dirty clothes into clean ones. Then I redressed the girls and combed out their hair as best I could.

When they were ready, Mrs. Dorset turned to me. "I will not be seen with you in that ridiculous outfit. You need to get rid of those clothes."

I thought about refusing, but then I realized it would do no good. The Dorsets owed me money, so I didn't want Mrs.

Dorset to get mad at me. My quilt had been tied behind me on the burro. I removed it and went off to change.

When Mrs. Dorset decided we were presentable, we started off for Panama. I didn't really think she would be able to walk that far, particularly wearing all those petticoats and her soft boots, but she never once complained. Edna and Harriet quickly became tired and cranky. Mrs. Dorset finally allowed the girls to ride, so we put them on a burro, and I walked beside them making sure they wouldn't slide off.

By the time we got to the gates of the city, my dress was so wet it clung to my back. When I complained about it, Mrs. Dorset told me that ladies never sweat, they "glowed." That sounded pretty silly to me.

We were barely through the gates before our guides unloaded our luggage, demanded their additional money, and then turned their animals around and headed back toward the mountains.

We found ourselves in a big square. From the distance the city had appeared clean and white, but on closer look most of the buildings were crumbling and many of the windows were broken.

Mrs. Dorset sat down on one of the trunks. "Are you sure this is Panama City?"

"Yes. Now you just stay here," Mr. Dorset said to us. "I'll go find the Pan America Export Company. Mr. Sanchez has arranged housing for us."

Malachi stood around for a few minutes, and then he

said, "I don't figure I'll be staying with the Dorsets. I'm going to look for some place to sleep."

I nodded. Malachi didn't move.

"Well?" he finally said. "I need money for a room."

All of our luggage was piled around our feet. I started to move the trunks around looking for my quilt.

"Are you hiding our money from me?" Malachi said.

"Not exactly," I said. "I don't trust some of those miners."

"I have to find a place to stay too," Kevin said. "I'll pay for Malachi, and he can pay me back."

I watched the two of them walk away. Kevin was a comfort to have around.

We seemed to be attracting attention. Men, women, and children had gathered around to stare at us. The little children looked very much like the children in Chagres. What clothes they were wearing had once been white but were now dusty brown. They were friendly but shy. When they saw Harriet and Edna looking at them, they covered their faces with their hands and then smiled and giggled through their fingers.

Harriet and Edna giggled back.

"Stop that!" Mrs. Dorset wiped her face with a handkerchief. "This heat will kill me. I shall die here, I just know it."

I was relieved to see Mr. Dorset returning. Following him was a short plump man wearing a wrinkled white suit. When he saw Mrs. Dorset sitting on a trunk, he let out a cry of dismay.

"This is terrible," he said in a heavy accent. "I have called for my carriage. You poor *señora*. My wife has been expecting you. Do not worry, in a few minutes you will be out of here."

"This is Señor Jesus Sanchez," Mr. Dorset said. "My new partner. We will be staying with him until the house he has found for us is ready."

In a few minutes we heard the sound of horses' hooves, and before long a carriage stopped in front of us. It was followed by several servants. They were dressed in loose white pants and tops and they were leading two horses.

Señor Sanchez helped Mrs. Dorset into the carriage. Then he reached down and picked up Edna. "You have beautiful daughters," he said to Mr. Dorset. Before he could pick up Harriet, she scrambled into the carriage by herself.

"Ah," Señor Sanchez said to me, "and you are the oldest daughter?"

I shook my head. I wasn't sure if I should follow the servants who were carrying the trunks down the road or if I should get into the carriage. While I didn't exactly think of myself as a servant, I was sure the Dorsets did.

Mr. Dorset said to Señor Sanchez, "She's not my daughter, but she has been a great help to Mrs. Dorset and the girls."

Señor Sanchez put his hand on my elbow and helped me up. Mrs. Dorset looked annoyed, but she moved over and made room for me on the seat.

Mr. Dorset and Señor Sanchez followed us on the horses.

The wall outside of Señor Sanchez's house looked as dilapidated as the rest of the town, but when we entered the courtyard, everything was neat and clean, with huge pots of colorful flowers everywhere. A short little woman ran out of the house making clucking sounds as she opened the carriage door.

She immediately started speaking to us in Spanish. Señor Sanchez dismounted and helped Mrs. Dorset out. "Welcome to our *hacienda*. I'm afraid my wife does not speak English, but my daughter does. She has just gotten back from boarding school. You shall meet her at dinner."

While we couldn't understand a word Señora Sanchez said, it was obvious she was kind. She patted Harriet on the head and shook her own head when she saw how tired Edna was. She led us across the courtyard and into the house. She clapped her hands, and almost immediately we were surrounded by chattering maids who led us up a flight of stairs.

In the middle of a bedroom was a copper bathtub filled with steaming sweet-smelling water. Before we could say anything, several of the women started to unbutton Mrs. Dorset's dress. I didn't think Mrs. Dorset would want me or her children watching her take a bath, so I took Edna and Harriet by the hand and backed out of the room.

Several maids followed us and then led us to another bedroom with a second copper tub. I undressed the girls and put them into the tub, and with the help of a young girl I washed them. While I was drying their hair, one of the women brought some clothes and another brought a tray with cookies and warm milk. I don't know who owned the clothes, which turned out to be nightdresses, but they fit the girls and were clean and soft. One of the maids turned down the covers on a bed, and after they had drunk some of the milk and eaten a cookie, I tucked Harriet and Edna in. They were already half asleep. The maid arranged some sheer material around the bed to keep the mosquitoes away.

The maids then tried to unbutton my dress, but I shook my head and shooed them out of the room. One of them left me a nightdress and a towel. I undressed and climbed into the tub. The water must have had something in it because it smelled of flowers and felt slippery on my hand. I leaned back and closed my eyes. I wiggled my toes and sighed.

When the water began to cool, I climbed out and wrapped myself in the towel that was on a chair. The night-dress was too short, but when I slipped it on, the material felt wonderful on my skin. I ate a few cookies myself, and then, although it was still light outside, I climbed into bed next to Harriet and fell asleep.

When I woke up, it was dark. Harriet and Edna weren't awake, so I quietly got out of bed and tiptoed to the door. I wasn't sure what time it was. I found a young maid asleep across the threshold. She leaped to her feet and indicated that I should stay where I was. I really hadn't planned to go wandering around the hall in a nightdress, so I waited while she ran down the hall. In a few minutes another girl came back with the maid.

I knew the girl wasn't a maid. She was wearing a silk

dress, and her thick, brown hair was arranged in elaborate curls. She was carrying an embroidered bright red shawl.

"Oh good, you are now awake," she said. "I have been so very anxious to meet you, but I was afraid you would sleep all night."

"You speak English?" I said.

"Yes, not perfectly yet, but I am so improving. I am Consuela Sanchez. If you feel up to it, we will be having dinner in a while. You need a dress, though. Come along." She handed me her shawl.

"I'm Molly Malarkey," I said, wrapping the shawl around myself and following her down the hall.

I tried not to stare when she opened the door to her room, but everywhere I looked there was something new to see. Piled on the bed were pillows covered in shiny material, and in one corner there was a kneeler in front of a statue of the Blessed Mother. The statue was dressed in a blue robe and had a gold crown on her head. Clothes spilled off the chairs.

"As you can see, I am very untidy," Consuela said. "But I have just come back from boarding school and my maid has not sorted out my things. Here, sit down." She gathered the dresses off a chair and dumped them on the bed. "I am so happy to see someone my age that I can practice my English on."

"Your English sounds all right to me," I said. "I can understand everything you say."

"Yes, but I am too formal, you understand? And sometimes, I have to think before I can find the right words."

I nodded. "Maybe you could teach me some Spanish?" I asked.

"But I know Spanish," Consuela said. "No, no, when I'm with you, we must only speak English. Besides, Mama does not know any English at all, so she will never comprehend what we are speaking about."

She pawed through the dresses on the bed and finally picked out a thin cotton one covered with flowers. "It is an old dress. I was going to give it to my maid, Rosa, but I think it will fit you. I do not know where your things are. Rosa said that they were all wrinkled and smelled terribly. In a few days you should have all your own things back."

"They took everything?" I said.

"If there is something you need, I will discuss it with my maid. What is it you want?"

"My bonnet, and a little sack," I said. I didn't care that much about the bonnet, but if my sack of money was gone, I didn't know what Malachi and I would do.

"I will inform my maid, and she will find the articles that are missing. But now we must see that you are dressed for dinner. Papa can become, how you say, obsessed about promptly serving food."

"He becomes angry if dinner is late?" I suggested.

"Yes, there, you see, you will be able to help me." She pulled some white undergarments from a pile on the floor.

"The nuns wouldn't let us have lace on our undergarments. You can keep all these plain petticoats and drawers. I don't think I will need them again. I am finished with boarding school."

I thought she would step out after she gave me the clothes, so I could change in private, but she made herself comfortable on the bed and kept talking. I was too embarrassed to take off the nightdress in front of her, so I changed by keeping it on and using it as a sort of tent. Only after I had the undergarments on did I pull the nightdress over my head.

Consuela laughed when she saw what I was doing. "The nuns would love you," she said. "They even made us bathe in our drawers and waists. They said we must always have people see us properly dressed. Nuns have strange ideas. Do you have any shoes?"

"I guess they're back in the room, where Harriet and Edna are."

"We don't want to wake them up," Consuela said. She went to her closet and finally found a pair of velvet slippers. "Your feet look bigger than mine, but these are old and have stretched out. Turn around." She sighed. "The dress is much too short, but that cannot be helped. Why are American girls so tall?"

I couldn't answer that, so I put on the shoes. I could feel my toes pushing against the front of them, but the material was so soft they didn't really hurt.

"*Bueno*. Come on now, I'm starving," Consuela said.

I wasn't sure if I was supposed to eat with the family. On the boat with the Dorsets there weren't any formal dinners, so I didn't know how the Dorsets would feel about me at the table with the Sanchez family.

When we arrived at the dining room, Mr. Dorset was already there. He stood up when the two of us arrived.

"You both look quite charming," Señor Sanchez said, bowing from the waist.

Mr. Dorset smiled at me as I sat down next to Consuela. When I discovered that Mrs. Dorset was having a light meal in bed, I relaxed.

"Molly is going to help me with my English, Papa," Consuela said.

"Excellent," her father said.

"Molly is on her way to California," Mr. Dorset said, "as soon as she and her brother can find passage on a ship."

"Well, we shall hope she changes her mind," Señor Sanchez said. "Perhaps she will find Panama a pleasant place to stay."

I didn't argue with them, but in spite of the good food and the friendly Consuela, I wasn't going to stay here. I was more than halfway to California.

10

I lived like a rich person in Panama City. In the Sanchezes' house there were servants everywhere, sweeping, cleaning, cooking, and running errands. All Consuela would have to do was clap her hands and someone would appear almost magically to find out what she wanted. Mrs. Dorset spent the first days we were in Panama in bed. The servants petted the two girls and fed them sweets and brought their own children in to play with them. For hours at a time I didn't have anything to do but visit Consuela and have her show me all her clothes and talk about how strict the nuns had been.

The Sanchezes had given Mrs. Dorset a maid, so I didn't have to worry about looking after her clothes or dressing her. But as she recovered from the trip, she called me to her bedroom to question me about what the girls were doing.

"You need to be with them," she said. "I don't trust those servants. I don't understand what they are talking about."

She seemed happier though; she enjoyed being treated like a queen and seeing her girls spoiled as if they were little princesses.

A few days after we arrived I took the girls for a walk. In the city square, I met Kevin.

"Where is Malachi?" I asked. "Is he staying out of trouble?"

Kevin shrugged. "I tried to get him to stay in the hotel I was at, but he didn't like it. Not that the hotel is very nice. I don't particularly care for sleeping in a small room with three or four men. They snore and fight all the time. And conditions are getting worse here. They get drunk and fire off their guns at all hours of the day and night. They have broken up some of the public festivals and tried to force the señoritas to dance with them. I'm afraid the men are not going to tolerate that kind of behavior."

"Do you think we'll ever get to California?" I asked.

"It's not going to be easy," Kevin said. "More and more miners are arriving every day, and most of them have tickets. I was down at the shipping company's office today, and none of the ships they have listed are on schedule. They're not returning from San Francisco. The sailors are abandoning them and going to the goldfields. And some of the ships scheduled to come to Panama are afraid to stop for fear of being mobbed."

"Are you saying we're stuck here?" I said.

Kevin nodded. "Not forever—but yes, right now we're stuck."

I slowly walked back to the Sanchezes' with the girls. I began to be afraid I would end up a servant forever.

I wasn't sure where I fit into the Sanchez household. Consuela acted as if I was a guest or a friend. Mrs. Dorset, in her usual way, considered me a servant and couldn't seem to understand why Consuela talked to me at all. Mr. Dorset was always friendly and didn't seem to have a problem with my eating dinner with the family, but he was gone most of the day on business. The Sanchezes were kind to everyone.

Mrs. Dorset needed Consuela, though. Consuela could tell her what the maids were saying, and then she could tell the maids what Mrs. Dorset was saying. My contribution was to explain to Consuela what Mrs. Dorset wanted.

I liked Consuela but we didn't have much in common. She couldn't seem to understand I had a job watching Harriet and Edna even when they were playing with the maids' children or riding ponies at the stable. In a way, Consuela was a lot like my friend Lucy back home. All she wanted to talk about was clothes and boys, especially Kevin. He was a dinner guest frequently. Mr. Dorset and Señor Sanchez both liked him.

"Are you and Dr. Doyle friends?" she asked me one day.

I looked at her. "Yes, we're friends," I said. "But we're not courting or anything like that. You know he's going to California?"

"Perhaps he would like to stay in Panama. I'm sure Papa could find him a job," Consuela said. "Maybe you will stay too."

I shook my head. "I don't want to work for the Dorsets forever," I said. "I could have stayed in New Hampshire if I wanted to be a servant."

"But you don't have to be an employee," Consuela said. "You can be my companion. Ladies don't work. Or you could marry one of my brothers. They will be coming home from school for Christmas."

"I don't even know your brothers," I said. And I could see that being Consuela's companion would be the same thing as being her maid.

"That doesn't matter," Consuela said. "I won't know who I am to marry. Mama and Papa will pick out the man for me."

I was shocked. "Is that how they do it in Spain?"

"I don't know," Consuela said. "I've never been to Spain. Do you think Dr. Doyle will come to our New Year's Night dance if I ask him?"

Knowing Kevin, I was sure he would come, although I didn't think he was exactly smitten with Consuela. She was my age, and he treated us like his younger sisters.

So much had happened, I hadn't realized it was so close to Christmas. We had never celebrated Christmas at home. Pa didn't believe in celebrating anything. We never had presents. Once, Ma made me a rag doll. She put it on my bed, so

I would find it on Christmas morning. I loved that doll, but after Ma died, one of my brothers threw it to one of our dogs, who tore it to pieces. When I ran crying to Pa, he told me I was too big for toys and that I should grow up. Besides, Christmas at home meant snow, dark days, and trees that were black, bare silhouettes. But here in Panama the days were warm and there were flowers everywhere.

After Kevin accepted Consuela's invitation, she started pleading with her father for a new dress. Then she tried to talk me into having a new dress too.

"I can't," I said to Consuela. "I need my money for California."

"I can get Papa to buy you one. When I beg, he will give me anything. Or I'm sure Mr. Dorset would buy you one."

"I don't think so," I said. I couldn't even imagine asking Mr. Dorset if he would buy me a dress. I knew I was poor, but I didn't like being treated as poor. And besides, I had the plaid taffeta Mrs. Needham had given me in Boston.

"I don't need a new dress. I have a perfectly good one," I said to Consuela. We were in her room. I was waiting for Harriet and Edna to wake up from their naps.

"Can I see it?" Consuela said.

The maids had cleaned and pressed my clothes, including the dress Mrs. Dorset had thrown away. They had returned my sack and bonnet. The bonnet was really beyond repair, but I was so relieved to have my money back, I didn't really mind. I tiptoed into the room I shared with Harriet and Edna and pulled the taffeta dress out and held it up against me. I had forgotten how pretty it was. But Consuela was not impressed. When I returned to her room, she fingered the skirt.

"It's nice material," she said, "but nobody wears this style anymore. Where did you get it?"

"Never mind," I said. I gathered the dress into my arms.

"Don't worry," Consuela said. "Manuela is a wonderful seamstress. She can remake it for you."

"It fits me fine," I said. "I'm not sure I want it changed."

"Of course you do." Consuela took the dress out of my arms. "It is fortuitous it has much material."

Before I could stop her, she sailed out of the room calling for Manuela.

Consuela got her new dress. It was white, and the skirt was covered with row upon row of ruffles. Around her waist was a scarlet ribbon. "And see," she said, modeling it for me in her bedroom, "on my head I will wear my *abuela*'s comb and her lace *mantilla*." She whirled around in front of me. "It is a tradition in my family that the daughter of the house wears her grandmother's comb. Do you think Dr. Doyle will like me in this?"

"I guess so," I answered. I had on my plaid dress—or what was left of it.

Manuela was crawling around the floor pinning up my hem. She suddenly made a clucking sound and leaned back on her heels.

"What is it?" I said. I looked down. Manuela pointed at Malachi's old boots that I was still wearing.

"You can't go to a dance wearing those terrible boots," Consuela said scornfully. "Why are you always wearing men's shoes?"

"I don't have any others," I said. "Besides, the dress is long, no one will notice."

"No, no, no. I will lend you a pair of mine," Consuela said.

But Consuela's boots were much too small. Her hands and feet were tiny compared to mine. That might explain why I always felt so awkward around her.

"Do not be concerned," Consuela said. "I will find you something. Perhaps one of my cousins has big feet."

I knew the old boots were a disgrace, but the dress more than made up for it. It was so grand, I thought, no one would look down. Manuela had done a wonderful job. It was the first time I had a dress that really fit me at the moment I would wear it. It seemed for the last few years that my clothes were always too tight or too short. Pa had refused to give me any money for new material, so I could only let out seams and patch holes with scraps of the boys' old shirts.

I stared in the mirror. This dress made me look like a lady.

When Mrs. Dorset heard I was going to the dance, she called me into her bedroom. Mr. Dorset was working at the desk— he looked up and smiled when I came in.

"I know this is a foreign country," Mrs. Dorset said, "and customs are different, but a servant attending a party as a guest doesn't seem proper to me. Are you sure the Sanchezes know you are going? Consuela may be overstepping her position as the daughter of the house. Besides, who will watch Harriet and Edna?"

"Nonsense," said Mr. Dorset. "I don't really consider Molly a servant. And she is entitled to have a little fun occasionally. There are plenty of maids who will look after the girls until they go to bed."

Mrs. Dorset started to protest, but Manuela came in carrying her dress, and Mrs. Dorset became busy criticizing the changes Manuela had made.

In the days before Christmas the house was filled with the spicy, pungent smells of cooking and the sweet odor of the flowers the gardeners kept bringing in. Maids were rushing about cleaning and polishing the floors and the furniture.

The servants had no time now for Harriet and Edna, so I always had them with me. But Consuela wanted to talk about her brothers and Kevin, and she didn't want to listen to Harriet and Edna, who kept constantly interrupting her.

One afternoon when we were in her room she complained to me. "Why can't they just go off and play by themselves?"

"They're my responsibility," I said.

"But my brothers are coming home today. I want you to meet them."

While I wasn't against meeting her brothers, I was afraid of how Consuela would present me. Knowing how single-minded she could be, I was worried she would propose I marry one of them the minute we met.

"What will you wear for dinner?" she asked.

"A dress," I said. When Mrs. Needham had given me four dresses, I couldn't imagine needing more. Now four dresses seemed a ridiculously small number. And I certainly couldn't wear the dress Mrs. Dorset had thrown away.

Consuela sighed. "But your clothes are so out of fashion, and you wear them over and over again. If only you weren't so big, I could lend you one of mine."

I refused to take offense. I knew I was taller than almost every woman in Panama.

"Perhaps I could lend you one of my lace shawls," Consuela said. "It will make your old dress look better."

I met her brothers, Alphonso and Felipe, at dinner that night, and I don't think it mattered what I wore. Even with Consuela's beautiful shawl, I didn't impress either one of them. I might as well have been Harriet or Edna for all the attention they paid me.

But they ignored Consuela too. They wanted to talk with their father and Mr. Dorset, and Señor Sanchez wanted to know all about their school. Even their mother could get their attention for only a few minutes before they went back to their own conversation.

After dinner the men left to have cigars and drinks in another room. Consuela explained that this was the custom. Señora Sanchez and Mrs. Dorset went into another room to have coffee. Consuela said it was very uninteresting there because all they would talk about would be housekeeping and things like that. Since Mrs. Dorset didn't speak Spanish, I doubted if they talked about anything.

I started to go upstairs to relieve the maid who was watching the girls.

"Which of my brothers do you like?" Consuela asked, following me up the stairs.

"How would I know?" I said. "Neither one said a word to me."

"But which do you think is the handsomest?"

"They're both nice looking," I said.

On Christmas Eve the Sanchez family went to midnight mass. Kevin brought Malachi, and the three of us went with the family. Mr. Dorset wanted to go. He thought it would be interesting, but Mrs. Dorset said she wouldn't go to a Papist mass and she didn't think it would look right if he went without her. The mass we went to was held in the largest of the many Catholic churches in the city. The church was filled with people. The Sanchezes had their own pew, which we were invited to share. The servants had to stand to the side against the wall. The church was lit with millions of flickering candles. Small boys wearing what looked like red dresses and white lace blouses marched down the aisle singing. One of the boys was carrying a metal dish with holes in it. He held it by a long chain, and when he swung it back and forth, sweet-smelling smoke came out.

"Incense," Kevin whispered.

At midnight all the churches in the city rang their bells.

After mass the family gathered in their parlor and drank hot chocolate. When I started to leave to go to bed, Consuela stopped me.

"Here," she said, handing me a box. "Usually we exchange gifts on the Feast of the Three Kings, but you will have need of these before that."

"But I don't have a gift for you."

Consuela ignored my excuse. "Open it," she said.

I untied the red ribbon and lifted the lid. I pulled out a pair of soft leather boots.

"Try them on," Consuela said.

"Here?" I asked.

"Yes, I want to be sure they fit. I tried to explain to the shoemaker what size you wore, but since you were always wearing those horrible boots, I had nothing to show him. If they don't fit, he said he would fix them before the dance. You cannot go to our dance wearing those awful shoes. What would people think?"

"They're beautiful," I said. I untied my old boots and slipped my feet into the new ones. I wiggled my toes. I never knew shoes could feel so soft. "They fit perfectly," I said. "Thank you."

Once Consuela had given me my present, she paid no more attention to me, so I excused myself and went upstairs. I was almost undressed for bed when I heard a knock on the door. It was Mrs. Dorset.

"I'm sure you're aware how late it is," she said.

"The Sanchezes invited me to have some hot chocolate," I said. "And Consuela gave me these boots. Aren't they beautiful?"

After looking at them, she said, "They are most impractical for someone in your position. This is a very foolish gift. I'm afraid Consuela can at times be a silly girl."

I refused to let Mrs. Dorset think I agreed with her. "She's been very nice to me," I said.

"Be that as it may," she said, "Consuela is quite out of your class, and she is putting inappropriate ideas in your head. I'm sure after thinking about it, you will return the boots."

There was no point arguing with Mrs. Dorset, so I put the boots back into their box for safekeeping. I had no intention of returning them.

"I think you had better get some sleep," she said. "The girls will keep you quite busy tomorrow." As she started out the door, she turned. "Oh, Merry Christmas."

11

A few days after Christmas, when all the food had been eaten, the cooks started preparing food for the New Year's dance. I watched as men carried huge sides of beef into the kitchen, where the cook cut them up with a cleaver. The air again smelled of strange spices. Floors that had been polished just last week were polished again. The maids shooed Edna and Harriet away, so most of my days were spent keeping the girls busy. Once Consuela saw I didn't have time to gossip with her or talk about how she should wear her hair for the dance, she stopped looking for me.

But on the day of the dance she did come to the stable, where Harriet and Edna were riding ponies.

"When Anita is through doing my hair, she can do yours," she said. "It must look special so my brothers will be sure to notice."

I reached up and touched my hair. I had never "done" anything with it before. I only washed it and tied it back. And I was sure that nothing I did with it would make her brothers notice me.

"Come to my room after my siesta," Consuela said.

When I brought the girls back to the main house, Mrs. Dorset was busy trying to explain to her maid what to do with her hair.

"Keep Harriet and Edna out of my way," she said. "I can't abide them today." She sighed. "Oh, what I would give to be understood. If you go anywhere, be sure to take the girls with you."

I wondered if she was deliberately keeping me busy so I wouldn't have time to get ready for the dance. Even if I wasn't interested in catching the eye of Consuela's brothers, I wanted to wear my dress and new boots and to look my best.

When I thought Consuela would be through with her nap, I took Edna and Harriet down the hall to her room. Consuela wasn't happy to see them, but after they promised to sit quietly, she allowed them to stay. I watched as Anita curled and arranged Consuela's hair. When she was finished, it was piled up high with ringlets. In the middle Anita placed Consuela's grandmother's fancy silver comb. It wasn't like any comb I had ever seen. It was quite tall and with a design of scrolls and flowers. Anita draped the *mantilla*, a square of lace, over the comb. Consuela stepped into her dress, and Anita pulled it up and fastened the back. She kept fussing with the neckline until Consuela pushed her away.

"You look beautiful," I said.

"Yes, beautiful," Harriet agreed. "I wish I was old enough to go too."

"Someday," I said.

Then Anita tried to arrange my hair. She made clucking sounds when she picked up a strand. She brushed it and tried to do what she had done with Consuela's hair, but Consuela had thick, smooth hair and my hair was wiry and went every which way. Anita muttered something in Spanish, all the time shaking her head.

"What did she say?" I asked Consuela.

"She says you should have wrapped your hair in rags so it would all go in the same direction. But it is too late to do that now. She says you have terrible hair."

Finally, Anita braided my hair, wound ribbons into the braid, and then wrapped the braid around my head. She tied the ribbon into a big bow at the back just above my neck. Then she pulled out strands so that they hung down around my cheeks. She kept poking hairpins into the braid to make sure it didn't come tumbling down. When she was finished, she held up a mirror for me to see the results.

I didn't look like me—at least, not as I thought I looked. The face staring back at me looked older.

I felt even older when Anita had me step into two stiff petticoats and then the taffeta dress, which rustled and swayed. The new boots had tiny heels that made me look taller. I had to walk carefully and keep my shoulders back so I wouldn't fall over.

Consuela was delighted. "Alfonso and Felipe will be overcome," she said. "You look so much better."

Even Mrs. Dorset gave me a compliment when I took the girls to her all dressed up.

"You look quite nice. Is that one of Consuela's dresses?"

"It's mine," I replied.

Harriet stroked my skirt. "You look like a fairy princess," she said. "Consuela looks like a bride, but I like your dress better."

I carefully leaned over and gave her a hug. "What a nice thing to say."

"I wish I could see all the other dresses," Harriet said.

"You're much too young to go to a ball," Mrs. Dorset said. "It's not a place for children."

"I just want to look," Harriet said.

"I tell you what," I suggested. "If it's all right with your mother, and if you promise to leave when I tell you, I'll bring you and Edna downstairs for a few minutes before many people are there."

Mrs. Dorset reluctantly agreed. "But only for a short while. By the time I'm ready, I expect the girls to be back here."

When Consuela saw the girls, she sighed and rolled her eyes. "Why are they still with you?"

"I promised they could watch the dance for a few minutes," I said.

While the girls ran ahead, Consuela asked, "Why did you do that? How can you dance if you have two babies following you around? We have to be early because it is my parents' party, but the girls won't stay very long, will they?"

"Of course not," I replied. "And you forget, I don't dance very well." Truth to tell, in spite of how I looked, inside I didn't feel any different, and I didn't think I would be very good at charming men.

As we came down the stairs, Harriet grabbed my hand. "It looks like fairyland."

The hacienda was filled with flowers, and all the candles had been lit. The central hall had been cleared of furniture for dancing. Along the wall there were tables heaped with food and bottles of wine.

"That is not the main meal," Consuela said. "We will have a midnight supper." She looked around. "Good, there are many people here already. Sometimes people don't come until it is very late. Then I feel so stupid just standing around talking to old ladies and cousins I don't even know."

When she saw Kevin, she went up to him. She used the fan she carried to cover half her face, so only her eyes were showing. "How do I look, doctor?" she asked, twirling around in front of him.

"Quite charming," he said, but I noticed he was looking at me. "Molly, I wouldn't know you," he said. Then he added, "You look so grown up."

"I'm the same age I was yesterday."

He laughed. "Dance with me," he said.

"Maybe in a few minutes. But I promised Harriet and Edna I would let them look around."

"Well then," Kevin said, "Harriet Dorset, will you do me the honor of dancing with me?"

Harriet giggled, but she allowed Kevin to pick her up and waltz her around the dance floor. When he brought her back, Edna pulled at his jacket. "Me next, me next," she demanded.

Kevin scooped up Edna and gave her a waltz too.

Many of the guests smiled as they watched Kevin and the girls. Only Consuela wasn't smiling. After their dance I let the girls go to the table and fill a plate with tiny cakes to take upstairs. The maid who was assigned to watch them was waiting.

"Their mother wants to say good night to them and talk to you," she said. The three of us went into their parents' room.

"We were hardly there at all," Harriet said to her mother. "I like dancing."

Mrs. Dorset, who was still fussing with her hair, turned away from the mirror. "What are they talking about? Who were they dancing with?"

"Kevin just waltzed them around the floor," I said.

"Well," Mrs. Dorset said, pulling on her long white gloves, "I am sure they are now overstimulated and won't go to bed."

"Yes we will, Mama," Harriet said. "See." She jumped onto her mother's bed, still wearing her dress and shoes.

"Very amusing, Harriet. Now take your shoes off the covers and go get into your nightclothes." She turned to me. "I shall expect you to behave in a manner befitting your station. It is only by the kindness of Consuela that you are going at all."

I wasn't sure what behavior would be befitting my station, so I simply nodded.

Mr. Dorset was waiting at the top of the stairs. I followed the Dorsets down.

"You look quite charming," Mr. Dorset said to me. "I'm sure you will be the belle of the ball."

I doubted that, but at least I knew I had one dance with Kevin, and I was sure Consuela would force her brothers to dance with me.

When Kevin saw me, he came over. "Now," he said, "shall we dance?"

"I'm not very good," I said.

Kevin guided me around the floor. He didn't act angry when I stepped on his toes. "Just relax," he said. "Nothing terrible is going to happen if you miss a step."

I started to relax and look around. I saw Consuela frowning at me over the shoulder of a man in uniform who she was dancing with.

"I think Consuela is jealous," I said.

"Of what?"

"She fancies you," I said. "Do you like her? I think she's pretty."

Kevin looked at Consuela as if he were seeing her for the first time. "Yes, I guess she is pretty, but she acts as if she is."

"What do you mean?" I said. "If you're pretty, how could you not act as if you were?"

"Because she only cares about how she looks—she doesn't care how other people feel," he said. "She is absolutely ignoring that soldier she is dancing with."

Kevin's comment took me by surprise. I didn't think men would notice anything like that. My brothers never seemed to care about anything but getting what they wanted. Kevin was different. Thinking about my brothers made me wonder what Malachi was doing. I suddenly realized I hadn't seen him for several days.

"How is Malachi?" I asked.

"He has an unfortunate habit of finding a wild group to run with," Kevin said.

"Was he caught cheating?"

"I hope not, but the sooner we leave Panama, the better," Kevin said. "I'm afraid there is going to be real trouble between some of the Americans and the Panamanians. The miners seem to feel they can do anything they want. They fight in the streets and have broken up a few dances in the square. The Americans are becoming very unpopular."

Before I could say anything else, the music stopped and

Consuela appeared at our side. "You owe me a dance," she said to Kevin.

Kevin bowed. "I'm always willing to dance with my hostess," he said.

"Oh, that would be Mama," Consuela said. "I'm too young to be a hostess. I am just here to have fun."

As another waltz started, Consuela turned to me. "Your dancing was not too dreadful," she said. "I will find my brothers to dance with you in a few minutes."

I moved quickly off the dance floor and stood on the side where the older women, most dressed completely in black, were watching the dancing. When they saw me, they put their fans up to their faces and chattered among themselves. I'm sure they knew I really didn't belong there.

Some of the dances were exciting to me, with much foot stamping and the couples standing and facing each other. When the first dance of that kind started, Kevin came over to me.

"I'm afraid dancing school didn't teach me that."

"You went to dancing school?" I asked.

"My mother insisted. I think she was trying to make a gentleman of me."

"You must have been very rich." I seemed to be constantly reminded of how poor my family was and how isolated our little village had been. "I never met anyone who went to dancing school."

Just then Consuela's brother Felipe came up to me. He swept his arm across his chest and then bowed deeply.

"Would the *señorita* do me the great honor of dancing with me?"

I almost giggled. But taking a deep breath, I nodded my head. Consuela told me later I should have curtsied.

Once on the dance floor, Felipe didn't talk to me at all. He kept looking around. When I missed a step, he would sigh and roll his eyes. The minute the music stopped, he brought me back to the side of the dance floor, bowed, and walked away.

I was looking for Kevin when a soldier asked me to dance. After him, another soldier danced with me. And then another. Some spoke English and others didn't; some looked angry when I stepped on their toes and others apologized. I began to feel almost dizzy from trying to understand them and to stay off their feet. When it was time to eat, Kevin reappeared. I almost threw my arms around him.

"You seem to be very popular," he said.

"I don't know why," I said.

"Now, Molly," Kevin said, "you know you look very nice—well really, more than nice—and why wouldn't a man think you're attractive? And since you're with the Dorsets, they probably think you're a rich American."

"So they are only dancing with me because they think I'm rich?"

"You know I didn't mean that," Kevin said as Consuela appeared.

"Come and eat with me," she said, taking his arm. "Oh, Molly, I think the Dorsets are looking for you."

I knew Consuela was lying, but I was tired of the dance anyway. While dancing looked like fun when I was watching, it was hard work when I was actually doing it.

"Good night," I said to Kevin. "Thank you for the dance."

As I went up the stairs, I turned and looked at the party one more time. Who would have thought back home that Molly Malarkey would attend a party like this, wearing a shiny dress that rustled when she walked?

12

One morning a few weeks after the dance Mr. Dorset came into the room where I was teaching the girls to do their letters. Edna was really too little to learn, but she wanted to do what Harriet did.

"Molly, I'd like to talk to you."

"Be good," I said to the girls, and followed him into a room he was using as an office.

"Are you still determined to go to California?" he asked.

"Yes," I replied.

"I want you to know you have been a very great help to us. And we'd be more than happy to have you continue to live with us and watch the girls. We would pay you, of course. Do you think you'd be interested in that?"

"I don't think so," I said. "There's my brother Malachi, and we are supposed to meet my father."

"I was afraid you would say that. So I have made certain arrangements—that is, if they meet with your approval."

I nodded and waited to hear what he had to say.

"Señor Sanchez tells me there is a Peruvian whaler nearby. They have already picked up a few Americans and Peruvians who are going to San Francisco at a port called Callao in Peru. But with all the confusion in Panama, they don't want to stop here. As a favor to Señor Sanchez, they will moor out of sight in the far side of the bay and accept a few passengers. But they obviously don't want it known they are here. I am willing to pay for your passage. Kevin will pay his own way. But then what about your brother?"

"I have some money to pay for his passage," I said. "I would be grateful if the whaler would take him too."

Mr. Dorset nodded. "Yes, it is probably very wise that he go with you. I have a feeling he and his friends are helping to create problems between the Americans and the Panamanians."

"When would we go?"

"In a few days. I don't think you should tell your brother until the last minute. From what I have heard, I do not think he is discreet. And I am afraid some of the Americans will get violent if they know there's a ship available that they can't get on."

I nodded.

"Now, here is the money I owe you. It is a good amount—perhaps it would be best if Kevin kept it for you?"

When I shook my head, he smiled and handed over the envelope. "You are a very independent young lady and quite presentable. So there is something else I'd like to talk to you about. To be honest, I don't have much faith in your brother watching out for you, and traveling with a young single man such as Kevin would seem to some people . . ." He picked up a pen and fingered the quill. "To be blunt, Molly, people might think you were not a respectable young lady." He looked at me. "Do you understand?" I could swear Mr. Dorset was blushing.

"Kevin has always behaved like a perfect gentleman," I said.

"Yes, yes, I'm sure he has. I just think you need to be careful. People will talk. Well now, that concludes our conversation. I suppose you had better tell Mrs. Dorset of your plans."

Mrs. Dorset couldn't believe that I was really serious about going to California. "But what will I do?" she said. "Really, this is most inconvenient. The girls have gotten very fond of you, and how can I find another nanny who speaks English?"

"Consuela might know someone," I said.

I hadn't seen much of Consuela since the dance. In a way, that was my fault. I knew she wasn't really interested in anyone but herself, and I was tired of her constant chattering about boys and clothes.

"I suppose I must learn Spanish," Mrs. Dorset said. "The house Señor Sanchez has found for us is ready, and I will have to manage the servants. And now I will have to worry about the girls too. This is very thoughtless of you. I'm very disappointed. I thought you were more dependable."

There was nothing I could say.

When I began to organize my things, I realized that carrying my belongings around in a quilt and always having to keep unwrapping it was too clumsy. At the market I found a straw valise. It seemed cheap enough, so I bought two, one for Malachi and one for me.

When Harriet and Edna saw me packing, they became upset. "Don't go," Harriet said. "Who will take care of us?"

"No, no," Edna said, pulling at my skirt.

"There are lots of people who will take care of you. And you have your mother and father."

"Mama says we give her a headache," Harriet said.

"Then you must learn to be quiet around her," I replied.

I thought Consuela would be angry when she heard Kevin was going with me, but when I told her, she seemed to have already forgotten about him. One of Alfonso's friends had come to visit, and she had taken a fancy to him.

"It is better," she said to me. "Mama and Papa would not want me to like an American. But I have come to give you a going-away gift." She handed me the shawl she had lent me when I first met her brothers.

"Oh, this is too pretty and I'm sure it was very expensive," I said.

"Do not worry. It is not as if it is a special shawl like the nuns at the convent make. So it did not cost so much. Besides, you could not take a fancy shawl to California."

"Thank you," I said.

The captain of the whaler had anchored far out in the bay to avoid anyone coming aboard against his wishes. On the night we left, Kevin and Malachi came to the Sanchez house with their luggage. I decided to wear my pants again since I knew I would probably have to climb aboard the ship. I kissed the girls goodbye and thanked Mr. and Mrs. Dorset. Mr. Dorset pressed some extra money into my hand.

"Be careful," he said.

One of Señor Sanchez's servants led us to a quiet beach outside of town, away from the main beach, where miners often gathered and slept. We climbed into a small boat, and the servants started rowing. Finally I saw the light of a lantern bobbing in the dark.

As we drew alongside the whaler, a sailor leaned over the railing and shouted something.

"What did he say?" I asked Kevin.

Kevin shrugged. "It sounds like Spanish, but it must be a dialect. I don't understand him."

There was a rattling sound as a net was lowered over the side. I stared at the whaler. I hoped I would be able to climb up the net without making a fool of myself or falling into the ocean. Kevin must have sensed how I felt.

"Malachi can go first, and you can follow," he said. "I'll be right behind you, so don't worry."

I nodded and watched as Malachi scrambled up the netting. I was good at climbing trees, I told myself. This couldn't be any harder. And at least I didn't have to worry about petticoats and skirts getting in the way.

"Come on now," Kevin said.

I wrapped my fingers around the netting, but getting my feet off the boat was hard until Kevin finally gave me a boost. Once my feet were on the netting, it was a little easier to start going up hand over hand. But I wished that the netting didn't sway so much.

Don't look down, I told myself. Below, Kevin was shouting, "You're doing fine, hang on!" From above, a sailor was yelling something to me, but I ignored him. Even though I couldn't understand him, I was sure he was telling me to hurry. My arms started to ache. I tried to look up to see how much farther I had to go, but changing my position only made the netting swing away from the whaler. I quickly went back to staring straight ahead at the side of the ship.

I began to think my arms would stop working when I felt someone grab my shoulders and haul me roughly up over the railing and dump me onto the deck. I scrambled to my feet.

"Didn't think you were going to make it," Malachi said.

I straightened my shirt and ignored him.

The sailor reached down and pulled Kevin onto the

deck. Kevin then leaned over and pulled up our luggage, which he had roped together. A man who I guessed was the captain because he was wearing a fancy blue coat covered with gold braid came over to us and started talking very fast.

"What's he saying?" I said.

Kevin shrugged. "I think he is saying we were late. I can recognize a word here and there."

"Can I help you, mate?" One of the sailors watching us stepped forward. I was relieved to hear him speaking English.

"Why is the captain angry at us?" I asked.

"The ship's already overloaded, and he didn't want to take you, and he wants to get away from here. You'll have to sleep in the hold, and you can't expect any special treatment."

I turned and looked at Kevin. Remembering how men had behaved in Panama, I didn't want to be stuck in a hold with the likes of them.

"Could you tell the captain that this one"—Kevin pointed at me—"is a girl? Perhaps he could find other lodging for her?"

The sailor looked at me more closely. I had tied my hair up to keep it out of the way and was wearing the cap. Maybe I had fooled him. The sailor started talking to the captain and pointing at me. The captain threw up his hands, shook his head, gave me a hard look, and finally said something to the sailor.

The sailor looked unhappy. "The captain said that is not

his problem, and if this female is stupid enough to go where she is not wanted, then she will have to take care of herself. Sorry, mate, but the captain is in a foul mood. He's sorry he ever decided to go to San Francisco at all. He's afraid that when we get there, all the sailors will jump ship and head for the goldfields. Come on, I'll show you the hold."

The hold was dark and smelly and filled with piles of luggage and men just sitting around. Both sides of the hull were lined with bunks. We dumped our luggage in the first empty space we saw.

"You can't dump your junk there. That spot is taken," a scruffy man said. He kicked my valise, sending it flying across the floor.

"What'cha think you're doing?" Malachi said. He balled up his fists.

"Sorry about that. Where is there an empty space?" Kevin had stepped in front of Malachi.

"Are you crazy?" I whispered to Malachi. "If you get into a fight, we could be dumped overboard."

"He didn't need to kick our stuff," Malachi said. But he backed off.

"Maybe under the bulkhead." The man pointed to a place in the corner with a very low ceiling. A supporting beam took up most of the area. "And keep your friend under control. Plenty of men down here have knives."

We picked up our bags.

"Mind the slop pails!" the man called after us, laughing in a nasty way.

The bulkhead smelled worse than the rest of the hold. It didn't help that several slop pails were stored there.

"Maybe you'd like to be our cabin boy and dump them overboard?" a miner yelled at me.

"Pay no attention," Kevin said. "If it's the cabin boy's job, then let him do it. We don't want to draw attention to ourselves."

We moved as far away from the pails as possible and settled down with our belongings arranged around us. Although we had the bulkhead to ourselves, I still worried about our safety. I was glad I had stuffed our money down the front of my shirt before coming aboard.

It was almost impossible to sleep in the hold. Besides the smell and the thick air, some men stayed up until all hours drinking and gambling. Others snored loudly. And then there were those who did nothing but fight and argue. At the first hint of light most of us couldn't wait to go on deck, where at least there was fresh air and a clean wind.

Even on deck we discovered we couldn't pick any place we wanted. Most of the men claimed a special spot and wouldn't let any other passenger use it. Some days when there was hardly any wind, the ship would roll from side to side, but it didn't seem to move forward. After a few days of going nowhere, the Americans became nastier than ever, starting fights and demanding that the captain do something or they would string him up. Fortunately, most of what his American passengers said, the captain didn't understand. He did understand their expressions, though. More than once he lost his temper, and then there would be less food to eat. This wasn't exactly a hardship since the food was terrible anyway, and the water tasted even worse.

After a few days we all smelled terrible.

"How long is this trip?" I asked Kevin.

"I heard it takes a month if the winds are good, but it can be longer depending on the weather."

I tried to find my own spot on deck away from most of the men and out of the way of the sailors, but often I would choose someone else's place by mistake.

"Move on, kid," they would say. "This spot is taken."

Once, because a miner thought I was moving too slowly, he picked me up and tossed me across the deck. I didn't want to draw attention to myself, so I picked myself up and didn't say anything.

Most of the time the trip was boring. There was nothing to do. Twice a day we lined up for food. The cook would dump our meals onto tin dishes supplied by the ship, and then we would go back to our space to eat. The sailors pretty much ignored us except when we were in their way, and then they would kick at us and order us off the deck. Just as it was below deck, the passengers' main activity seemed to be gambling and complaining. Malachi was completely happy. I knew there was no way I could keep him from playing cards, so I just ignored him. Kevin was busy making friends with the sailors and trying to learn their dialect of Spanish.

———

One day Frank, the sailor who spoke English, came over to me as I was sitting on deck.

"The captain wants to talk to you."

"I haven't done anything," I said. "Besides, how can I talk to the captain? We don't speak the same language."

"Come along, I'll translate."

The captain was in his cabin. He barely looked at me but immediately started talking to the sailor.

"What's he saying?" I said.

"The cook's boy is sick, and the captain wants you to help out."

"Why?" I asked.

"He says you can sleep in the storage locker in the kitchen if you will do this."

I thought for a minute. "All right," I said. Nothing could be worse than the bulkhead, and at least I would have some privacy and something to do. I was tired of sitting on the deck and looking at the sky and water. "I'll go get my clothes."

Kevin seemed relieved that I would no longer be sleeping in the hold.

Frank came with me to the mess and introduced me to the cook. He was fat, with a droopy mustache and a dirty apron. He didn't look very happy when he saw I was a girl. He pointed to a locker in the corner and indicated I should put my belongings there.

"Is this where I sleep?" I asked Frank. He nodded.

At the beginning of the voyage, I imagined, the locker

had been full of supplies. Now, aside from a few sacks filled with food, the floor space was empty. But with my quilt I decided I could make it comfortable.

The cook waved a large soup ladle at me and pointed to a pile of limp, tired-looking vegetables and made a chopping motion. I picked up a knife and examined the vegetables. I recognized the carrots and potatoes, but there were some I had never seen before. I shrugged and began to work.

My job seemed simple enough. The cook never said anything to me. He just pointed at what he wanted me to do. After a few days he started laying out the food I was to prepare and then he would leave. When he came back, he would dump the vegetables I had cut up into a pot of water. There was always a fire going on the stove, but he indicated that I was not to touch it. I had never seen such terrible food. The vegetables were wilted, and the potatoes had black spots and were growing sprouts. The sacks of flour he used to make the bread were full of weevils. And the small supply of salted pork was infested by maggots. The cook would bake bread twice a week. After a day the new loaves were infested too. At mealtime, when the cook would bring out the loaves of stale bread, he would hit them on the side of the table. I watched in horror as bugs would crawl out and drop to the floor, where the cook would casually step on them. Once he showed me how to pick the maggots out of the meat before it was put into the stew pot.

After a few days he became more friendly. He would actually smile at me, and once he patted me on the shoulder. In a way, I was happy. While I didn't wish the boy bad luck I hoped he wouldn't recover until the trip was over. Now I had something to do and a safe place away from the miners. I worried about the supplies, though. I didn't know how much longer our trip would take, but there didn't seem to be much food left. I hated to think how the miners would behave if their meals got even scantier.

One day I was peeling potatoes when the ship started to sway and roll. A pot skittered across the stove. I made a grab for it, when the cook suddenly burst in and pushed me roughly aside. He removed the pot and doused the fire, then turned on me and began to yell. I didn't know if he was telling me to stay or to go, but he looked so angry I dropped my knife and backed out of the galley.

On the deck there was total confusion. Sailors were running everywhere, and the miners were being herded back into the hold. I gasped when I saw the size of the waves spilling over the deck. The air was heavy, and the sky had turned gray. The wind was blowing so hard, it pushed me against the railing.

Kevin suddenly appeared at my side. "Get below!" he screamed at me.

I hesitated for a minute, and then I fled back to the galley. I didn't want to be down in the hold if the ship began to sink. The cook was busy lashing everything that could move to the walls. When he saw me, he pointed to the pots that were spinning across the floor and then indicated that I should put them in the cupboard. I braced myself against the wall, grabbed pots as they skittered by, then tried to shove them into the cupboard. Finally everything in the galley was secured. He then grabbed me by the arm and shoved me ahead of him out of the galley and into another small room. He pushed me under a table that was bolted down, and then he disappeared. I had no idea where he went.

I don't know how long I crouched there. At times it felt as if the ship was being ripped apart. The wind screamed and water beat against the porthole. At one point I was afraid the ship was upside down. Another time there was a terrible crash. The ship tilted and I slid from under the table and banged against the wall. As the ship righted itself, I crawled back under the table. After what seemed like days but was probably only hours, the wind finally stopped howling. The ship was still rolling. When I got to my feet, if I hung on to the wall, I could walk across the floor. I was almost afraid to go out on the deck—I might find I was the only one left alive.

13

The ship was a mess. It looked like a giant hand had picked it up and shaken it. The deck was covered with broken pieces of crates and luggage. One of the water barrels had split in two. Part of a mast was blocking a passageway, and a group of sailors were already dragging it away. Other sailors were furling the sails that were ripped and hanging limply. I picked my way across the deck looking for Kevin and Malachi. When I saw them near the railing, I went over.

"I was afraid something might have happened to you both," I said.

"The ship was lucky," Kevin said. "No one was killed, and only a few have been hurt. I hear a sailor broke his leg when he fell from the rigging, and some of the miners are complaining of bruises."

Suddenly I was grabbed from behind and swung

around. It was the cook. He pushed me across the deck and into the galley and indicated that I should start cleaning up the mess. He got the fire going, found one of the big pots, filled it with water from the barrel stored in the galley, and set the water to boiling. The door to my storage locker was hanging open, and what was left of the food supply was scattered all over the floor of the galley. I started to sort through the vegetables. As fast as I could chop, the cook grabbed the ingredients from me, tossed them into the pot, and stirred. After a while he filled a bowl from the pot and gave it to me.

"Sailor," he said, and slapped his leg.

I guessed he was talking about the sailor who had broken his leg, but I wasn't sure where the sailor was. I shook my head.

The cook pointed to the door and gave me a shove. Carefully carrying the bowl, I went out and looked for Frank.

"I think this is for the sailor with the broken leg. Do you know where he is?" I asked Frank when I found him.

He led me to the sailor's quarters. "I better bring it in," he said. "I don't think the sailors would like a woman in their quarters."

I handed him the bowl and ran off. I was afraid the cook would be mad at me if I was gone too long. When he was angry, which was often, he would grab me by the collar and shake me.

The storm seemed to have scared the miners. In spite of the fact that the meals were worse, the water supply was rationed, and much of their luggage had been swept overboard, they stopped complaining and threatening the captain.

After the storm the sky became blue with only a few white clouds. Wind filled the mended sails, and the ship seemed to almost fly over the water. According to Frank, we were making good time. It was a relief when we started to see land birds in the sky. Finally one afternoon the captain ordered all miners on deck. Frank was there to translate what he said.

"We should reach San Francisco in a day. Have your belongings assembled on the deck as soon as possible."

Immediately the miners fought their way below to sort out their remaining possessions.

In the middle of the night I was suddenly awakened by a loud grating noise. I sat up, terrified that we had run into something. I pulled on my pants and shirt and crept out.

"Move back, miss," Frank said when he saw me. "We're dropping anchor."

"Are we there?" I said. It was so foggy, it was hard to see.

"We're anchoring out near the Farallons. That pile of rocks over there," he said. "We need daylight and clear skies to enter the bay. But it could stay foggy for days."

I nodded and went back to my cupboard. I lay awake

for a while. We were here, I thought. We were in California. I couldn't believe the journey was over.

In the morning fog still hung over the ship. It was so thick that the top of our tallest mast was invisible and when I leaned on the railing, no matter how hard I looked, I couldn't see anything on the horizon.

"How far out are we?" Malachi asked. He and Kevin came over to stand next to me. "Can we swim to shore?"

"I wouldn't try it," Kevin said. "We don't know what the current and tides are like. Besides, we can't even see in what direction the land is. For all you know, you could start swimming out to open sea."

It was afternoon before the wind picked up and the fog drifted away and we could finally see San Francisco Bay and the city. The miners all rushed to the side. Even the cook was there, watching for the city to appear. I wasn't sure exactly what I expected. The way everybody talked of San Francisco, I thought it would be a big city. But the bay was so full of ships, it was difficult to really get a proper view. All I could see were a few houses climbing up the steep hills.

"It doesn't even look like a town," I said to Kevin.

"I imagine there are more buildings down by the waterfront that we can't see," he said. "But it's a fairly new town, so I don't imagine there are many permanent structures there."

The minute the miners could see the town, they demanded that the captain immediately enter the bay.

"He'll go when the tide and the wind are right," Frank translated what the captain said. "Just be sure you have all your trappings ready to disembark."

"Need any help?" Malachi asked me.

I looked at him suspiciously. "Who's mad at you now? Are you hiding from someone?" I asked. "I don't understand why you can't keep friends. Do they think you were cheating them?"

"Just hard losers," said Malachi.

"There must be a reason people are always thinking you are cheating them."

Malachi shrugged. "Anyway, I almost went crazy sleeping with all those men. Where's all your junk?"

"Come on," I said, leading him to the galley.

The cook looked up and frowned when he saw Malachi following me. I knew he didn't like strangers in his galley, but there was nothing he could do to me now.

"So this is where you slept?" Malachi said when I showed him my cupboard. He kicked at one of the sacks.

"Better than that bulkhead." I gathered up my clothes and the boots that Consuela had given me. They were so pretty and soft, I couldn't bear to wear them. I put them into my straw valise. I hoped Malachi's old boots would last me for a while longer.

"Are you going to keep running around in those stupid clothes?" Malachi said, pointing to the pants and shirt that were beginning to look the worse for wear.

"I haven't decided," I said. It was hard to tell which

clothes would be the safest. On board ship, where I couldn't get away and my skirts would be a bother, it was an easy choice. But in San Francisco I wasn't sure if men would take advantage of a girl or protect her. I thought maybe I would ask Kevin. Meanwhile, I put my valise back in the cabinet.

"I can manage this myself," I said to Malachi.

He shrugged and wandered out.

The cook had left the galley, and when he returned, he shoved something into my hand and then left again. I opened my hand. In my palm was a necklace with a pendant that had a carved whale on it.

When I showed it later to Kevin, he said, "Scrimshaw."

"What's that?" I said.

"Carving on whales' teeth. Lots of sailors carve these on long trips."

"I didn't even think the cook liked me," I said.

Kevin laughed. "Don't think so little of yourself."

Just when it looked as if we would enter the harbor, suddenly the fog descended again. The miners started cursing and yelling threats at the captain.

Again the captain sent Frank to talk to them. "The captain said that when the weather is clear, we will enter the bay," Frank informed the miners. "And if you keep fighting and yelling this way, he'll leave the bay and dump you all somewhere else."

That bit of information silenced the men.

The next morning the fog looked thinner, and by nine o'clock there were already breaks in the cloud cover. By noon we could again see the city. There was talk that we would be landing in the late afternoon.

I went back into my cupboard for the last time and changed into my oldest dress, the one I had worn to Boston. I decided that being a girl in San Francisco might be safer than pretending to be a young boy. During the journey I must have lost weight, because now the dress hung loosely on me. I shoved the pants and shirt into my valise and went onto the deck. The sailors were pulling up the anchor and unfurling the sails. The captain yelled at Frank, who yelled at the miners to stand back and get out of the way.

One of the miners came over to me. "Pardon me, miss, I think I should warn you. Your brother owes money to several miners. If he doesn't pay them, they're planning to get the money one way or another. If you get my meaning. I'd pay his debts if I were you."

I wasn't surprised. "I'll pay," I said. "Where are these men?"

When the men told me what Malachi owed, I was sure they were lying, but I didn't argue with them. They scared me. I gave them most of what Mr. Dorset had given me. Maybe I had made a dreadful mistake, bringing Malachi out here.

"What was that all about?" Kevin asked me when I went back to the railing.

"It's not important," I said. Kevin thought badly enough of Malachi; I saw no reason to make him think worse.

Leaning on the railing, I could feel the ship's sails capture the wind. The deck shuddered, and then the ship began to move forward. There were so many ships anchored in the bay, ours couldn't get near the docks. The captain had to wedge the ship between a sailing ship and a steamboat. The lifeboats were lowered, and the miners began to fight to get a place in the first boat heading to shore.

Malachi tried to get Kevin and me to push our way into the boat.

"A few minutes more won't matter," Kevin told him.

Just then Frank came over to us. "The captain says if you want to stay on board tonight, you're welcome to do so. It will be dark soon, and going ashore in the morning will give you time to find lodgings."

"That sounds very sensible," Kevin said.

Out of the corner of my eye I could see Malachi edging toward the railing. "Malachi would never wait," I said to Kevin, "but you can stay here."

"I don't know if it's safe for you," Kevin replied. Then he said to Frank, "Tell the captain thank you, but we'll go ashore now."

"Suit yourselves," Frank said. Then he grinned. "I'm planning on jumping ship. Digging for gold sounds better than staying on this tub and chasing after whales. Have you ever smelled whale blubber being boiled? Enough to turn your stomach, it is."

Once we landed on the dock, we were almost knocked over by the mobs of men who filled the streets. The sidewalks were wooden planks laid on top of mud. People had dumped rotting food and discarded junk into the middle of the street. Some of the junk looked like the mining equipment our shipmates had been dragging with them from Boston. Horses and carts splashed mud up onto the sidewalk, making it slippery and smelly from the spoiled food and the horse manure. There was a lot of shoving and yelling. I had gotten used to hearing Spanish since sailing from Boston, but now I heard dozens of languages. The whole scene was deafening.

The docks were lined with buildings that advertised drinking and gambling. Others were restaurants or hotels—most had signs saying they were filled. Many of the places were really just large canvas tents with wooden fronts facing the street. Only a few were wooden all the way through. The backs of most were canvas.

"Is your father supposed to meet you in San Francisco?" Kevin asked.

"No, in his letter he told us to see somebody called Barney. I don't know if that's the name of a tavern or a man or what."

"You're the one who's supposed to be so smart," Malachi said to me. "Just how do you think you're going to find this Barney?"

"If you were by yourself, Malky, I suppose you would know where to go?" I said.

"Children, children, enough of that," Kevin said. He took my arm. "If we don't find Barney tonight, we will tomorrow. I think we need to see if there's a place to stay first."

"It don't matter to me where we sleep," Malachi said. "We need to figure out where Pa and his gold is."

Suddenly a man stepped out of the dining tent next to us and rang a bell. "Dinner is served!" he yelled. "All you can eat!"

"Shall we stop and have dinner?" Kevin said.

"We don't have time," Malachi objected.

"It will be dark soon," Kevin said. "How do you expect to find anybody in the dark?"

Malachi grunted.

The restaurant was an open tent with no sides, just a roof. In the center of the space were long wooden tables and benches. The men on the street started to make a mad rush for places until they noticed I was a girl. Then one of the men elbowed others aside and cleared a place for me.

"Sit right here, miss," he said. He kept others from grabbing the spot until I sat down.

Malachi quickly took advantage of the man and grabbed the seat next to me before the man could sit down, then moved away from me to make room for Kevin. Some of the men grumbled at Malachi, but then the platters and bowls of food were dumped in the middle of the table and everyone reached for them and paid no more attention to Malachi.

The food was terrible. There was a bowl of beans with bits of fat swimming on top, a platter of beef that was dark and curled up on the edges, and a plate of potatoes with black spots. Before we could start eating, a man came around and demanded three dollars.

"Three dollars!" I objected. If food was going to cost us this much, we would soon run out of money. I dragged out my valise, which I had put under the table, and rummaged around for the purse I kept our coins in.

"Don't let people see how much you have," Kevin whispered.

I covered the purse with my skirt and, when no one was looking, I poked around until I found nine dollars.

"I see you haven't been to the mines yet, miss," the man who was collecting the price of the dinner observed. "Hard coins are rare nowadays."

I noticed that most of the men at the table were paying with flakes of gold or nuggets. The man collecting the money took the gold over to a scale on the counter and weighed it. Sometimes he returned some of the gold to the diner, and other times he indicated that he wanted more.

"I'll pay you back," Kevin said when he realized I had paid for his dinner.

"You've earned it watching out for Malachi," I whispered after making sure Malachi couldn't hear me.

Before long, it was clear that having a girl at the table was embarrassing for the men. The minute one started to tell a story, another would nod in my direction and the man's voice would fade out.

"Begging your pardon, miss, but where are you bound for?" the man sitting to my left asked.

"I'm looking for my father," I said. "Have you ever heard of a man called Barney?"

"Not that I recollect," he said. "But I've only been here for a day or two. Hey, fellows, any of you know of a gent called Barney?"

There was a general discussion, but nobody seemed to have heard of him. Finally one man said, "Try Connelly's pub up the street and over a block. He's been here for almost six months. He knows everybody."

"Let's go," Malachi said. "This food isn't worth eating anyway."

"At three dollars I think we should eat our fill," I said. Malachi grudgingly agreed, but when the main dinner was replaced by some kind of pudding, he shoved his plate away.

The pudding was gray and lumpy, so we did the same thing and left. We followed the directions the man had given us and quickly found the pub. It was a wooden building with a swinging door. When the customers saw a girl entering the place, there was a moment of silence. We went up to the bar.

"Looking for work?" the bartender asked me.

"No, she's not," Kevin said. "She's searching for her father. Have you heard of anyone named Barney?"

"And why would she want to find a thief like Barney? Are you Barney's daughter?" The man leaned over the bar. "If you can sing or dance, I can offer you a job," he said.

I backed away.

"Keep your ideas to yourself."

I turned to see who had said that. A large woman was standing behind me holding a laundry basket under one arm. "Can't you see she's a nice girl? Come along, lass, you have no business in the likes of a place like this." She took me firmly by the arm and pushed me out of the pub. Kevin and Malachi followed.

"I'll return your laundry in two days," she called back to the bartender. She smiled at me and then looked at Malachi and Kevin. "And who would be these fine fellows?"

"My brother and a friend," I answered.

"Come on, then. This is no town for a young miss like yourself to be wandering in. I can put you up in my house, and your brother and your friend can stay in my barn."

I couldn't help but wonder why she was being so helpful to us. I took a sideways look at her. She was almost as tall as Kevin but probably weighed more. Her face was red as if she had been sitting in the sun, but I couldn't imagine there was much sun in February. She glanced at me.

"You can trust me," she said. "Ask anyone. The widow Parnell is an honest businesswoman."

14

By the time we had hiked up a hill to Mrs. Parnell's house, it was dark. Her cabin had three rooms and a dirt floor. She took us through the kitchen into a tent attached to it where she had set up laundry tubs. Here she put down her basket. Lines holding drying clothes were strung all over the room.

She felt one of the shirts on a line and shook her head. "It's a chore getting the clothes dry with all this fog and rain," she said. "But the summers aren't much warmer. The fog is something fierce. Now then, what are all your names?"

"I'm Molly Malarkey, and this is my brother Malachi and our friend Dr. Doyle."

"Pleased to meet you. I'll tell you the arrangements. I have a barn out back that I've turned into a bunkhouse. Not much, but it's dry, and there is a mattress and a blanket for each man. Two dollars a night or fourteen for the week. If you pay for only one night, I won't save the bed for the next night. You have to be sure to come back early enough to claim a bed. If you pay fourteen, I'll save it for you. Come along now."

She lit a lantern and took us out the flimsy door in the canvas wall of the laundry room to a falling-down barn.

"It don't look like much, but the roof is sound," she said. "I don't serve food. Too many places in town do that. I make coffee in the morning, though. That's free."

Kevin and Malachi looked around the barn.

"I don't know how long we'll be here," Kevin said. "Perhaps for now, we'll pay the two dollars for one night."

"Fine with me," Mrs. Parnell said.

"Come along," she said to me. "You can sleep in the kitchen. As I said, I don't do cooking for the likes of them men, only a cup of coffee in the morning to speed them on their way, so I don't need the kitchen very early. But I don't see many young ladies, so . . . ah, well, sometimes I feel charitable. I'll give you all some breakfast. Nothing special, mind—I wasn't expecting company for breakfast. I have eggs and fresh-baked bread. One fifty a head for breakfast."

"Fresh eggs?" said Kevin. "We haven't had those in what seems like months."

"I have a nice flock of chickens out back, though I have a terrible time keeping people from stealing them. Heading for the goldfields, are you?"

"Right away," Malachi said. "We can't waste time here."

"Don't be silly," I said to him. "We don't even know where to go."

We went back into her main room, where we had dumped the luggage.

"You always think you know everything," Malachi said. "Well, pay her, I don't care. I'm going to find me the best bed." He picked up his valise.

Kevin handed Mrs. Parnell his money and followed Malachi out, carrying his bags.

I dug the bag of money out of my skirt pocket. Although Mr. Dorset had arranged for my passage on the whaling ship, I had had to pay for Malachi's trip and also his room and food in Panama and then today his gambling debts. If it hadn't been for my wages and Mr. Dorset's generous gift, I would have already spent most of Mrs. Throckmorton's money, and we would have practically nothing.

When I gave Mrs. Parnell the money, she took only the coins for Malachi.

"I can always use help," she said. "If you want to lend a hand with the ironing, that will pay for your lodging and food. From the looks of you, I don't see you eating me out of house and home. Now take some advice from me, lass—don't let that brother of yours keep taking advantage of you the way he is. A great lazy lout of a boy, if you ask me. Never even offering to pay his share."

Malachi was becoming a chore. He had done nothing to earn any money. If he won anything gambling, he certainly wasn't sharing it with me. I wouldn't be surprised if Kevin helped him out when we were in Panama. But I couldn't just turn him loose. I knew he would get into serious trouble. And I had promised Ma. I wondered if she realized what a burden she had placed on me.

"Are you short of money?" Mrs. Parnell asked.

"Not yet," I said, "but I'm not sure what it will cost to get to the goldfields. First, we need to find a man named Barney, who knows where our father is."

"If you want some honest advice," Mrs. Parnell said, "going to the goldfields isn't the way to make money."

"Have you tried it?" I said. "Hunting for gold?"

"My late husband was itching to go panning and to get rich the easy way. So we trekked up to the goldfields. Take my word, ironing is much easier than standing in freezing water and shaking sand to find little specks of gold. I told Jimmy, if you want to get rheumatism from wet feet, that's your concern. It's not for the likes of me, though. So I came back here, and I realized men were sending their dirty laundry to China! China! Can you imagine that? Filling ships with bundles of smelly, dirty clothes and then waiting months for the clothes to come back. Now that is just plain nonsense. So I found myself a nice stream of running water and went to work. My family wanted me to go back home to Boston when Jimmy died, but by then I had me a paying business. And I'm still here. I'm my own woman, none of that nonsense about taking care of my sister's children or doing housework for some lazy wife."

As I followed Mrs. Parnell, I told her we had been in

Boston for a while and my mother, when she was a girl, had once worked for rich people there.

"Well, will wonders never cease," she said as she handed me two blankets from a cupboard. She told me I could sleep on the kitchen table. "It's the best I can do," she apologized.

It was hardly more comfortable than the cabinet in the whaling ship's gallery, but at least I could stretch out.

Even though it was rainy and foggy outside, the kitchen was warm. I spread one blanket over the table and rolled up the other for a pillow. I didn't undress since I didn't know how much privacy I would have. I did take off what was left of my boots. No matter how little money we had, I needed to get some sturdy shoes. Since my feet had long since stopped growing, I decided I could buy a pair that fit me.

In the morning I helped Mrs. Parnell make huge pots of coffee to send her other boarders on their way. The men lined up outside her laundry door.

"Be sure to give them just two cups of coffee each," Mrs. Parnell said to me. "That will wake them up. I don't want them hanging around all day."

After the others had left, she scrambled eggs and offered home-baked bread along with the coffee to the three of us. "I'm not doing this all the time, but since Molly and I have come to a business arrangement, I'll be generous."

When Kevin and Malachi had finished, she shooed them out. "Be off with you. Go into town and try to find this Barney person. We have work to do."

I realized that I was part of the "we."

"Is there anywhere I can buy boots?" I asked. I held up my foot.

"Lord bless us," she said. "And how long you have been traipsing around like this?"

"Too long," I said.

"Not many businesses in town," Mrs. Parnell said. "Mostly gambling dens and drinking establishments. Everyone goes to the mines. Let me think now. The northern mines are still snowed in, so some men will be hanging around waiting for the weather to clear in the mountains. Seems to me I remember a Mr. Harris who stayed with me for a time. Said he was a cobbler back home. I haven't seen him lately, but he may be staying elsewhere. When I deliver my laundry, I'll ask around."

She set up the ironing board in the kitchen and placed the irons on the stove. "The men aren't too fussy about the backs of their shirts, but you need to pay attention to the collars and cuffs and those ruffles in the front."

"Ruffles on men's shirts?" I said.

"Gamblers, luv. You can spot them a mile away. Dandies they are, and that particular how their sleeves are, since they wear them fancy vests. If you see just a plain shirt, don't fret how smooth it is. Men who wear those kinds just want something sweet-smelling."

I was glad it was winter and drizzly outside because having the fire going to heat the irons made the little kitchen sweltering. I finally opened the door to cool the room with the wind that seemed to be always blowing. The stack of clean wrinkled shirts seemed endless. I didn't think I could iron them all in a week, and I was sure tomorrow there would be a fresh batch.

It was fine for Mrs. Parnell to have her own business, but it seemed to me she was just doing the same thing she was doing when her husband was alive, only now she was getting paid for it. But then I had done the same thing with the Dorsets. Maybe it was enough to get paid for work. But shouldn't women expect more? It certainly didn't seem fair.

I had been ironing for hours when Mrs. Parnell came home. She seemed pleased with the amount of ironing I had done. "Good lass," she said. "And I've tracked down that Mr. Harris. He's willing to sew you a pair of boots. He needs to measure you, though. Better run along and see him before he's off to the mines again. Down the road, and turn left at the tree that has a split trunk. There are five or six tents in a row. He's in the third one."

Before I went, I asked if she had found out anything about Barney.

"Now there is another problem." Mrs. Parnell set her laundry basket on the floor. "I have heard rumors that he's in jail. I didn't have time to go find out. Maybe tomorrow."

"That's not necessary." Kevin came through the kitchen door. "Can I come in? I found him. He's working at a bar over near the wharf."

I suddenly noticed that my brother wasn't with him. "Where's Malachi?" I said.

Kevin shrugged. "One minute he was beside me, and then he saw somebody he knew from Panama, and he was gone."

"So, " I said, "did you talk to this Barney?"

"A very shady character. At first he didn't want to talk to me. I don't think he trusts me."

"Maybe I should see him," I said. "I do have the letter."

"He's going to want money," Kevin said.

"Money? Why does he want money?" I said.

"Don't give any man money," Mrs. Parnell said. "Especially one you don't even know."

"How do you know he wants money?" I said.

"Because he said it will cost you if you want to know where your father is."

"Don't let this man bamboozle you," Mrs. Parnell said. "Come along now, I'll break my rules and fix us a little supper. Tomorrow you can go see the man. I'll go with you if you like."

"I'll be fine," I said. Mrs. Parnell might mean well, but there wasn't really any reason why I should trust her. Besides, she could be very bossy, and this Barney might take offense and not tell me anything.

After supper I went down to see Mr. Harris, who measured my feet and promised me he would have my boots in a few days.

"Be sure they're sturdy," I said.

Malachi had not come home by the time all the beds in the barn were taken. I woke up in the middle of the night to the sound of him banging on the door.

"Molly!" he hollered. "Let me in."

Before I could do anything, Mrs. Parnell stormed into the kitchen.

"There are no beds left," she said. "Go away."

"But it's me, Malachi."

"That's of no interest to me," she said. "If you're not early enough to claim a bed, that's your concern. Now move along and stop banging on my door."

"But where will I go?" Malachi said.

"That's your problem."

I sat up on the kitchen table.

"Now, don't you go feeling sorry for him," Mrs. Parnell said to me. "It's time he grew up."

I doubted if Malachi was going to grow up very fast, particularly in San Francisco.

In the morning Kevin and I went to find Barney.

"He was staying at the Union Hotel last night, but I have a feeling he doesn't stay anywhere very long," Kevin said.

I had expected to see Malachi sleeping on the ground outside, but there was no trace of him. "Where do you think he went?" I asked Kevin.

"Don't worry, I imagine he found a card game and spent the night."

Barney wasn't at the Union Hotel, but a man there said he had seen him going to the French Café for breakfast. The French Café was a canvas tent down the street.

"There he is," Kevin said, pointing out a large man standing at the bar. He had stringy hair that fell to his shoulders and a sagging belly.

"Mr. Barney?" I said.

All the men who were still eating turned toward me.

"Hey, missy! Want to come and keep me company? I'll let you blow on my dice," a man at a table called out to me.

I looked around the room. Half the men were eating, and the other half were playing some game where they were throwing dice.

I ignored them and went up to Barney. "I want to talk to you."

"That so?" Barney said. "I don't believe I know you." He slowly looked me up and down.

"I'm Malarkey's daughter."

"Oh yes, you sent that young man around to get my secret."

"What secret?" I asked.

"Now if I told you that, it wouldn't be a secret, would it?"

"My father told us to see you when we got to San Francisco," I said. "I don't think it was for no reason. From his letter, I think you know where he is."

"If I do, I'm not sure I should just be blabbing that to anybody. How do I know who you are?"

"I have the letter," I said.

"Oh," said Barney. "And where is that letter? I'd like to see it."

"I'm sure you would," I said. "But I don't think I trust you."

"And well you shouldn't," the man who was cleaning the table of breakfast dishes said. "Barney here is a bad lot. If you're looking for Malarkey, he said he was heading up to some Mexican town called Sonoran Camp or Sonora. That was a couple of months ago. I told him he was crazy to go in winter, but he wouldn't listen. If you ask me, Barney here don't know any more than that."

Barney frowned at the waiter. "Stay out of my business," he said, "or I'll make trouble for you."

"You don't scare me," the waiter replied. "My brothers can take care of your kind."

I looked at Kevin. Between Barney and the waiter, I trusted the waiter. He wasn't asking us for any money.

"How do we get to Sonora?" I said to him.

"You can take a boat to Stockton, and then I guess you can hike it. Not you, miss, but a strong man with a mule. Or if you have money, then I guess you can hire a wagon, but the road is pretty rough in places. There's creeks and rivers all along there that might have gold, and, of course, you can dry-mine. Are you thinking of hiring someone?"

"I don't think so," I said. "But thank you very much."

As we walked back to Mrs. Parnell's, I said to Kevin, "If I could hike to Panama, and cook on a whaler, I don't doubt but that I could get to the mines. Pa wasn't exactly in tip-top shape when he left for California."

"So you're still planning on trying to find your father?" Kevin said.

"Of course, that's why I came out here. And there's Malachi. Maybe the mines will be a better place for him. I'm afraid San Francisco is his idea of heaven and my idea of hell, for him anyway."

Kevin burst out laughing. "Do you mind if I tag along with you? Since Malachi is with us, I think it will be perfectly acceptable, socially speaking that is. I'm sure you know by now that I will behave like a perfect gentleman."

"I never doubted that you would," I said. "Thank you. And you know you're more than welcome. I think the sooner we get to Sonora the better."

"Why don't I go down to the wharf and see about arranging for a boat," Kevin suggested.

"Do you need any money?" I reached into my skirt pocket for my money purse.

"Molly, I told you before that it's not a good idea to let people see how much money you're carrying around," Kevin said. "Put the purse away. You can pay me back later when we're alone."

I watched Kevin go off down the street. There seemed to be nothing he enjoyed more than finding out things and making arrangements.

When I got back to Mrs. Parnell's, she was hanging another load of freshly washed clothes on lines that she had strung between the laundry room and a tree. "Hello, lass," she said. "With this wind, the clothes will dry outside today. They smell better than when I dry them in the house."

I told her what I had found out.

"So you'll be off then?"

"As soon as possible."

"Well now, it just seems to me you could have a pretty arrangement here. I was thinking. I can understand how washing and ironing might not appeal to a comely lass like yourself, but you know what else is needed?" She paused.

I shook my head.

"A seamstress."

"I don't think I'd be very good at that," I said. "All I've ever done is mend shirts."

"Oh, lass, lass, don't you see? Here you have a chance to do something on your own, be independent. As far as being good at sewing, most of these men won't know the difference."

"I know," I said. "But I don't think I want to do household chores, even if I am getting paid for it. And I can't let Malachi wander around by himself. I have to find my father, so I know Malachi is safe, and besides, I have a loan to pay back."

"You could pay the loan back by working here," Mrs. Parnell said. "And I'm not sure Malachi can be saved by your father."

I knew Mrs. Parnell was right, particularly about Malachi. But at least my conscience would be at peace if I left him with Pa. Pa had some control over him. I didn't seem to have any.

"Well," said Mrs. Parnell, "I can see your mind is made up. And if you're bent on doing this, then I suspect you need to get it out of your system. Remember, though, I will probably be here for a while, so always feel welcome to come back."

"Thank you," I said. Mrs. Parnell was kind, and she meant well. And in a place like this I decided I needed all the friends I could get. I suddenly gave her a hug.

15

When Kevin returned, he had Malachi with him. Malachi must have won money gambling because he was looking uncommonly cheerful. He even teased Mrs. Parnell a little, saying he would go to sleep now if that would assure him a bed.

Mrs. Parnell was having none of it. "That's all very well and good," she said. "But money will get you more than charm. Pay for the bed, and it's yours for the night." She held out her hand.

Malachi looked at me in confusion.

"Come, come, now, don't look at your sister. I've no doubt your pockets are filled with ill-gotten gains. You're a big boy. Pay your own way."

To my surprise Malachi fished some gold flakes out of a bag in his pocket and laid them in Mrs. Parnell's hand. She bounced the gold in her palm for a minute, and then she said, "Unless you want me to rout you out in the middle of the night, I'll take that much again."

Malachi dug into the bag and put some more flakes in her hand. She nodded.

"Better learn to weigh your gold, boy," she said. "Some people will think you're trying to cheat them."

Malachi muttered something, and then he slouched off toward the barn.

"Did you find out anything?" I asked Kevin.

Kevin sat down at the kitchen table. "It sounds pretty expensive and complicated. We have to find a boat that's going up San Francisco Bay, and then we arrive at someplace called Suisun Bay. The San Joaquin River empties into it. We follow the river to a town called Stockton, and then we hike inland from there."

"More boats and walking," I said. "Knowing Pa and how lazy he is, I'm beginning to wonder if he ever got to the mines."

"This is a big country," Mrs. Parnell said. "Not crowded like back home. It's easy to get lost out here. Even if he got this far, you may never find him."

"But I would think he would be looking for us," I said. "After all, he did send a letter telling Malachi to come out."

"Just Malachi?" Mrs. Parnell said.

"He didn't say I shouldn't come."

Mrs. Parnell shrugged.

"The good news is that there's still snow in the northern mines, so there aren't as many miners traveling as there will be in the spring," Kevin said. "We shouldn't have too much trouble finding a boat to take us to Stockton. Besides, we are going east. But there can still be snow."

"How soon can we leave?" I asked Kevin.

"First I have to find a boat," Kevin said. "And, of course, there has to be room on it. I'm sorry, but I'm going to need some money for you and Malachi. Things are far more expensive here than I thought they would be."

"Of course," I said. "And if we owe you any money for other things, I want you to tell me. There's no reason you should pay anything for us."

"It's been a big help going with you," Kevin said. "Without Mr. Dorset and his influence, I might still be sitting in Panama."

That night, after everyone had gone to bed, I sat down at the kitchen table and counted out the money we had left. If we were careful, we should be able to get to the goldfields. Once there, with luck, we would find Pa. And hopefully Pa would have all the gold we needed. But deep down I doubted that. Even if he had found gold when he wrote that letter, that was months ago. Knowing Pa, both the gold and the mine could have easily been lost.

In two days the cobbler had my boots ready. When he slipped them on and fastened the buttons, I wiggled my toes. I felt incredibly pampered. The boots didn't slide off my feet, I didn't need to stuff the toes with paper, and the soles didn't have holes in them. I didn't wear them while I was ironing, though. The kitchen was warm, and I was comfortable barefoot.

Kevin finally found a captain, a Mr. Webster, who owned a sloop.

"He's planning on taking a load of lumber to Stockton day after tomorrow, and he's selling spots on deck for the miners."

"How much?" I asked.

"Sixteen dollars a person," Kevin said.

I agreed. It sounded expensive, but at least it would save days of walking.

"I better go back and pay for our places," Kevin said after I gave him the money.

Mrs. Parnell washed all our clothes for nothing and even gave me a few extra dollars for my work because she said I was a good ironer—much better than her previous girl, who only wanted to sing and didn't like housework.

Mrs. Parnell also packed a food basket for us. "You never know if those thieving captains will have any food for the passengers at all."

Although the sloop wasn't due to sail until daybreak, Kevin thought we should show up the night before. When we got to the docks, there was a mob of men waiting. The sloop had anchored far out in the bay since the wharf was crowded with large sailing ships abandoned by their crews. A small boat was being used to ferry us out to the sloop. Men were pushing to get on it. A sailor was shouting that only people with tickets could get on board. Kevin pushed us forward, waving our tickets. The shouting sailor made room for us to get on.

"I'll be back for you if you have a ticket," he said to the crowd. "The rest of you need to find another boat going up the bay. Ours is full."

We shoved off, and the boat maneuvered between the larger ships, narrowly missing some and scraping the side of several. When we arrived, I found the sloop was a small boat with only one mast. What we seemed to have paid sixteen dollars for was a couple of feet on the deck.

"Grab three spaces on the deck, and don't leave them until we set sail," Kevin said. "If we lose our place, I'm not sure we could find another."

I wedged my valise under my legs and sat hunched over, trying not to be knocked down when men tried to get past us. In the dark, it was difficult to see anything. When the first streaks of dawn lit the sky, the sailors pushed us aside so they could get to the sails and hoist them. As the wind filled the sail, we headed up the bay. Fog drifted around us. Some of the men had brought jugs of liquor, and by afternoon many of them were drunk, and whenever they got up, they fell over everyone.

"Lucky you put on those boy's clothes," Kevin said. "With the mood these men are in, I don't know how they would treat you if they knew you were a girl."

In the middle of the day, the sloop suddenly shuddered. I heard a grinding noise and the boat stopped.

"What's going on?" somebody shouted.

"Ran onto a sandbar," one of the sailors said. "We'll have to wait until the tide floats us off."

"When'll that be?" another asked.

But the sailor had disappeared.

"I wonder how often this happens?" Kevin said.

I swatted at a flying insect and shook my head. At least we were sitting down. But it seemed as if the minute our sloop stopped moving, a horde of insects descended on us.

"Mosquitoes," Kevin said. "These look big enough to eat us alive."

"How about giving us something to eat?" the miner sitting next to us yelled at a sailor. "I thought you were offering us passage to Stockton. My understanding is passage includes food."

The captain came over. "I never promised anything, but I'm sure the sailors are willing to share some of their stores with you."

Most of the sailors started to protest, but the captain merely raised his hand and their complaining stopped. In a few minutes the cook came on deck carrying a large pot. A little boy followed with bread and bowls. The two passed among the miners, the boy giving each man a bowl and a slice of bread, the cook slopping something from the pot into the bowl.

"I don't know why we have to eat this swill when Mrs. Parnell packed us perfectly good food," Malachi complained.

"We don't want the others to know we have food,"

Kevin said. "I'm afraid some of the men wouldn't hesitate to kill us for a good meal. They certainly would try and steal it. Besides, I think we should save our supply."

I used the bread as a spoon. "It could be worse. Do you really think we are eating the sailors' food?"

"Probably there's plenty of food; the captain is just trying to save money," Kevin replied.

The cook's boy came by a little later and collected the bowls.

After lunch I watched several sailors, with long poles, try to rock the sloop clear of the sandbar.

"What will happen if they can't get us free?" I asked.

"Eventually the tide will free the boat—they're just trying to help it along," Kevin replied.

By now it had started to rain. First it was just a light drizzle, but then the wind came up and it became a downpour. At least the mosquitoes disappeared and the rain seemed to be helping free the boat. By late in the day we were again moving up the bay. There were hills on both sides that came down to the water. As we crossed the bay, we entered what looked like the mouth of a river, but it turned out to be the entrance to another bay.

"Suisun Bay," Kevin said.

The water here was rough. With the rain and the fog that seemed to be coming up from the surrounding land, it soon became difficult to see. The sailors were constantly peering over the railing to make sure the sloop wasn't going to get stuck on another sandbar. One time the boat was so close to the bank that the sailors could reach out and push the boat away with their pole.

When it became dark, the sloop was anchored near the shore.

It was impossible to lie down on the crowded deck, so I wrapped my arms around myself and tried to go to sleep.

The next morning the captain told us we were making good time, and in two or three days we should be in Stockton.

"Two or three days?" Malachi said. "I thought we'd be in Stockton in a day."

Most of the miners weren't exactly happy to hear this, either, and I couldn't blame them. It was obvious that the captain or somebody had oversold the small boat. Even with half the people on board, we would have been crowded. And as the wind and rain began again, the ship started to rock in the rough water. When the cook and his helper came around with the food, I noticed many of the miners refusing it. Malachi was one of them. I remembered how sick he had been on the *Meridee*. Since I hadn't been seasick then, I didn't hesitate to take a helping of the gruel that was our breakfast.

As the day wore on, the water in the bay became rougher, and men were hanging over the side throwing up. I was sorry they were sick, but it did give the rest of us the chance to stretch our legs and get a little more comfortable.

On the second day we crossed another bay and entered the mouth of the San Joaquin River. The waters of the river were quieter, but the mosquitoes had gotten larger and hungrier, the miners angrier, the sailors meaner, and the food scarcer. When no one was looking, the three of us ate most of Mrs. Parnell's food.

"This," I said on the third day, "is worse than anything else we've gone through."

"We must be almost there," Kevin replied.

"I think we could have walked faster," Malachi said.

In the afternoon we sailed into a small harbor. There were already a few ships moored there, some much bigger than the sloop we were on. And in front of us was the city of Stockton. The buildings hugged the harbor. Away from the river, the town just petered out with only a few scattered tents here and there. It was even more unfinished than San Francisco. There were only a few wooden buildings that seemed permanent.

We hung on to our luggage and let most of the other passengers get off ahead of us. It wasn't worth being trampled to death.

"Better get moving," one of the sailors said. "We have to unload the lumber, and then we have to take on the passengers for the trip back to San Francisco. When the miners find out there isn't as much gold as they thought, we bring them back to Frisco."

I wasn't surprised. After listening to Mrs. Parnell, I realized that gold wasn't just there for the picking.

The dirt streets were muddy from the recent rains. We

splashed down what looked like the main street and finally stopped at a tent that was advertised as a restaurant and hotel. But when we asked the price of staying there, the man at the counter said, "No room. You can eat or drink, though, if you want."

"Any rooms anywhere in the town we could rent?" Kevin asked.

"Not likely, when the ships are here. In a few days, though, most of the men will have left for the mines, and then I can give you a bed."

"Well," I said, "we can always sleep on the ground if we have to. It couldn't be more uncomfortable than the sloop. I think we should see if anyone knows of Pa."

We moved up and down the street, stopping at every establishment that sold either food or spirits. At the third place, a bar called Bill's, we asked the man behind the counter, who said he was the owner, if he knew of somebody called Malarkey. The man looked at me.

"Just one man?" he asked.

"No," I said. "His son, too, and maybe a third." I suddenly realized I had forgotten about Mr. Throckmorton.

"Wait a minute." The man turned and stared at Malachi and Kevin before he went behind a curtain.

When he returned, he was followed by a young Mexican girl.

The girl looked at us, then turned to the man and started to talk very rapidly in Spanish.

"She asks if you know where he is," the man said to me.

"Of course not. Why would we be asking about him if we knew? Who is this girl?"

"Her name is Rosalie, and she is the wife of one of your brothers."

"Matt," I said. So this was the singer Matt had married, I thought.

"Does she know where they are? Why isn't she with them?" I asked.

"Because they just disappeared, that's why, and he took all the money she had saved," Bill said.

I looked at Rosalie. She looked at me and scowled.

"She is very angry," Bill said. "She says he is very bad, and that he and his father are thieves."

"Does she know where they were going?" Kevin asked.

"No, they left without telling anyone, and she was afraid to follow them by herself," Bill said. "Rosalie is a nice girl. She has been helping me out, and she deserves better than being abandoned. I must warn you, though, she has many brothers in Mexico, and when they find out what happened to their sister, anybody called Malarkey had better be careful."

"Was there another man?" I asked.

"Not that I saw," Bill replied, "although your father did say something about a friend of theirs going on ahead."

"Where is this place called Sonora?" Malachi asked. "That's where we heard Pa was heading."

Kevin and I turned and frowned at Malachi, and Kevin jabbed him in the ribs. "Be quiet," he said.

Both Kevin and I were thinking the same thing. These people could be telling lies. Maybe Pa had really struck it rich and these people were planning to steal it. Or maybe they were planning on robbing us, although they wouldn't get much.

"Sonora?" Rosalie said. She started talking quickly to Bill.

"She wants to go with you," Bill said. "She says as Mateo's wife, she has a right. You are her only family here, but some of her family is in Sonora."

In Spanish, Kevin asked her a few questions, and when he finished, he whispered to me, "I think we can trust her."

"Why?" I asked.

"Just a feeling. Besides, we have nothing she could steal. And your father said that Matt had gotten married. How would she know that?"

I shrugged. We didn't have much choice. Since she could always follow us, it would be better if she were with us. Then we could keep an eye on her. And I felt very sorry for her being married to Matt. He was too much like Pa. I couldn't imagine why she would want to find him. If he had left her once, he would be likely to do it again. But that wasn't really my business.

16

Bill offered us a place to sleep. It was just a corner of a tent that was filled with boxes. He gave us some old sacks that were damp and smelled of mildew to cover the dirt floor with.

"You know," said Kevin as he started to lay out his burlap material, "the thing I miss most is a soft bed and clean sheets, warm blankets, and a pillow."

I can't say I ever had pillows or a soft bed. My mattress at home had been stuffed with corn husks that rustled when I turned over and smelled when they got wet because our roof leaked. But Bill's storeroom was no worse than the cook's locker or Mrs. Parnell's kitchen table. And sleeping there was certainly better than sitting up for four days on the sloop.

It was raining when we woke up. We gathered our things and went into the bar. Bill asked if we were ready to leave. "Looks like the rain has settled in," he said. "I've got some canvas sheets you can cover yourselves with, and you'll need a donkey or a horse. Trying to carry all your stuff is foolish. Just wear yourselves out. Better now than in the summer, though. The heat's like to kill you. One hundred and ten in the shade. Fact is, it has killed some and made others turn back. It'll be cold on the trail now, but at least it's too low for it to snow. If you're going up in the mountains, that would be a different story. But Sonora is at the bottom of the foothills and should be clear of snow. I'll see what I can do about a donkey."

"You've been awfully kind to us," I said.

"I'll be honest," replied Bill. "Your taking Rosalie will be a relief. I feel sorry for her and all, but looking after her has been a chore, I can tell you. Some of the men around here are anything but gentlemen."

He left us thick strong coffee and some griddlecakes. When he returned, he was leading a sad, bedraggled horse with a swayback and runny eyes.

He shrugged his shoulders. "The best I could find."

"This ain't no donkey," Malachi said.

"Take it or leave it," Bill replied.

"How much?" I asked.

"Thirty dollars," Bill said, "and that's the bottom line."

"Did you get something on the side?" Malachi asked.

"You have a smart mouth, kid. I'm doing this as a favor to Rosalie. I think she's gotten a raw deal, and I don't want to add to her burdens."

"I'll pay." I started to search for my purse.

"I'll split it with you," Kevin offered.

Rosalie came in. She had a striped shawl wrapped around her head and crisscrossed around her body in a way that left one arm free. She carried a straw basket and a guitar that she put on the floor. She looked upset when she heard Malachi and Bill arguing. I smiled to let her know we weren't angry at her. I wished she could speak English. It would be so nice to be able to share things with her. I had always wanted a sister to talk things over with.

"This horse belongs in a glue factory," Malachi complained.

"He's old," Kevin replied. He went up and examined the horse. "His eyes are infected, but I think I can clear that up by cleaning them. I can't do anything about his swayback, but if nobody tries to ride him and we're careful what we put on his back, he should be all right."

"If he can't carry stuff, what's the point of buying him?" Malachi said.

Bill seemed about to lose his temper. "Look, son, if you don't want the horse, just say so, though I don't see you offering any money to help pay your share. Are you prepared to carry your luggage?"

"All I'm saying is that there must be a better horse or donkey out there," Malachi argued.

"Tell you what, son. If you can find a better horse or donkey, I'll pay the difference."

"Never mind." I didn't want Malachi wandering

around because, sure as shooting, he would find a card game. "We've bought this animal, and we'd like to leave as soon as possible."

Bill packed us some food, which we paid for, and then he drew a rough map, which he gave to Kevin.

"It's a long walk," he said. "But this time of year it isn't too bad. Be sure you have warm blankets, and you better bring water. In summer you could die of thirst, but even now, unless you have your own supply, you'd have to pace yourselves to make sure you're near water when you get thirsty."

"Any idea where we can find blankets?" Kevin asked.

Bill turned to Rosalie and talked to her in Spanish.

She nodded and then gestured for us to follow her.

She took us to what appeared to be the Mexican section of town, stopping at a tent that had blankets piled out in front. Rosalie picked out four. After arguing with the man, she nodded at Kevin. He held out his hand with money in it, and she picked out some coins and gave them to the merchant.

She then found a potter who was sitting outside his tent surrounded by clay jars.

"*Por agua,*" she said to us.

I paid for two.

When we got back to the tavern, we filled the jugs with water from the pump. I named the horse Ben Two in honor of the horse we had left in Boston. Kevin washed his eyes. Then Kevin and Bill loaded as much of our luggage on Ben's back as we thought he could handle, and Bill showed us how to balance the water jugs on either side. The rest we would carry.

"Well," said Bill, "if I was you, I'd start now. Even if you don't get too far today, at least you've made a beginning. And there ain't nothing around here except ways for that kid brother of yours to get into trouble."

I agreed.

At first the trail was clear and level. Aside from the rain and wind, it wasn't hard walking. Remembering what Bill had said about water, we found a stream to follow. But we weren't alone on the trail. Several groups of men who didn't look very friendly passed us. They were grim-faced and did a lot of yelling and swearing and waving their rifles around. Some of them yelled taunts and rude remarks at Rosalie. If they thought someone was getting in their way, they would simply push him off the trail. When we saw how they were acting, we dropped behind but we could still hear them.

"Sometimes I wish I had a gun," Malachi said.

I shivered. "No, Malky. Terrible things can happen with guns." I thought that if I couldn't trust him with money, I certainly wouldn't trust him with a gun. "If we don't bother them, why should they bother us? We have nothing they would want to steal."

"There's the horse," Kevin pointed out.

"Don't make me laugh," Malachi said. "Who would want this nag? We walk faster than he does."

"He's old and tired," I said. "But he's better than nothing."

"If I had a gun, I could shoot us some rabbit for dinner," Malachi said.

I hadn't seen any game near the trail, but I was sure there was probably some hiding in the underbrush.

After we had been walking for a few hours, Kevin called a halt. "I think we should stop for the night."

"It's not dark yet," Malachi said. "What'd we go, a couple of miles?"

"If we keep on, we could get caught in the dark with no safe place to make camp," Kevin said. "I don't trust some of the men we've seen."

Malachi looked around. "This is safe? Anybody can see us."

Kevin pointed out a rock formation a few steps off the trail that would keep anyone from attacking us from the back, and would protect us from the wind. And the site gave us a clear view of anyone on the trail.

"I don't think we're going to be attacked," I said. "If we mind our own business, we should be all right."

Kevin disagreed. "Look, there are only four of us and—don't take offense—two of you are women. Admittedly, we don't have any equipment anybody would want. But some of those men sound crazy. Let's face it, they might just want you girls."

I almost laughed. After spending four days on the sloop, one night in a storeroom sleeping on a moldy sack, and hours walking for miles in the rain, I was a mess. But Rosalie still looked tidy. While she had said nothing, there was a quietness about her that was peaceful to be around, and for some reason she just didn't look as bedraggled or dirty as the rest of us.

Malachi dumped his bundles on the ground. "Couldn't you have found a place with trees? At least then we could keep a little dry."

"And get hit by lightning?" Kevin said. "No thanks."

I thought Kevin was being overly cautious. I hadn't heard any thunder or seen any lightning.

We unloaded Ben, and then Kevin led him to a stream near our camp. When Ben had drunk his fill, Kevin washed his eyes out again and tied him to a bush near some grass. Now we needed a fire. Most of the kindling out in the open was wet, but Rosalie and I finally found some twigs under the rocks. They were slightly damp, but Kevin managed to start them smoldering. We slowly added more twigs, and finally we had a decent fire.

Bill had given us canned beans. Kevin used his pocket knife to open one. There was also a package of round flat bread that Kevin said were tortillas. One by one Rosalie heated several of them in a flat pan, and we wrapped them around our beans. Bill had packed some coffee, and to our surprise we discovered he had included a pot. I dumped the coffee into it and added water from the stream.

"Do you think it's safe to drink?" I asked Kevin.

"The stream looks clear and it's running fast, so I would

think it's safe," Kevin said. "We can only hope. But make sure the water boils."

By the time we had eaten and cleaned up our campsite, it was getting dark.

"I think Malachi and I need to take turns standing watch," Kevin said.

"Why?" Malachi asked.

"I think one of us should stay awake to make sure nobody tries to steal anything. Why don't I take the first watch, and I'll wake you in three or four hours?"

We rolled ourselves up in our blankets and snuggled close to the rocks for protection. I slept for a while, but when I heard Kevin shake Malachi awake, I tried to stay awake. I was pretty sure Malachi would fall asleep again. When he started to snore, I quietly got up and, dragging my blanket, went to where he was half sitting, half lying on the ground.

It was useless to wake him up, so I settled myself on the ground to take the second watch. If Kevin was right and a man tried to get Rosalie or me, I could always scream. A scream would wake even Malachi.

It was nice to sit in the dark. Nobody wanted me to do anything, and it gave me a chance to think. It was hard to believe it was already the end of February. I had been gone from our farm since October. In a way, I guess I could say my dream had come true. I had gotten off our farm. I had found out that I could earn my own money. But in other ways, things hadn't changed that much. I was still doing the same chores women did all the time. I had learned I didn't want to watch other people's children because then I would have to take orders from their parents. Mrs. Parnell was smart to start her own business, but I really didn't think I wanted to wash other people's dirty clothes all my life.

But what did I want to do? My grandmother had come from Ireland all alone, but then she married right away. I wondered what she would have done with her life if she hadn't married the sailor she met on the ship. Of course, she had been widowed and she had my mother, so she had to worry about taking care of her. Not much different from me, I thought. I had Malachi to worry about. Except that Malachi wasn't a little child, he was eighteen. And it wasn't as if I was in charge or anything. I knew one day I would wake up and he would be gone, and there wouldn't be anything I could do about it.

I kept saying I was trying to find Pa, but to be honest, why? Deep down I knew Pa didn't want to see me, and he sure wasn't going to share his fortune with me—that is, if he had a fortune to share.

I suddenly sat up straight. Something was moving in the bushes.

"It's just me," Kevin whispered. He came out and sat down beside me. "I wanted to check up on Malachi. Why are you out here? We were supposed to be guarding you."

I pointed to Malachi snoring away. "I don't mind, and besides, it's peaceful out here."

"It's a beautiful country, isn't it?" Kevin said.

I looked up. It had stopped raining, and the clouds must

have broken up because I could see stars. "I suppose," I said. I hadn't really noticed. If I had to describe California to somebody at home like Mrs. Throckmorton, all I would be able to talk about was the dirt, the fleas, the mosquitoes, the crowds of yelling, dirty men, and all the walking we had to do.

"But, Molly," Kevin said, "it's wonderful. It's big. And we can go for days before we find another town, and then it won't be a real town, but just a few tents and maybe a wooden house."

"That's beautiful?" I asked.

"Of course, it's a new world. It's like everybody here is starting over and building everything new. We can become whatever we want."

I turned to him. "Does that mean you're not going to be a doctor anymore?"

"Maybe. But being a doctor out here would be different than being a doctor back home. There I'd be old Dr. Doyle's nephew, and it would be years before anyone stopped calling me young Dr. Doyle and trusted me with their grippe and broken bones."

"So are you going to start being a doctor out here?" I said. I was getting confused.

"I don't have to decide right now," Kevin replied. "We haven't reached our destination yet, have we?"

I gathered my blanket around me. "You mean Sonora?"

Kevin smiled. "Wherever. Think of all the new things there are to learn out here."

"You like to learn, don't you?"

"Don't you?"

I fidgeted with a twig. "Well, I thought I did. I did fine at school, and the teacher said I could be a teacher if I wanted to, but Pa made me quit."

"You don't have to be in school to learn," Kevin said.

I laughed. "Keeping house for the likes of my brothers and father didn't leave me much time. Pa didn't believe in having books around the house. And besides there wasn't any money to buy them."

"I bet that teacher would have lent you some."

"He did when I was in school," I admitted. "But after I left school, I never tried to borrow any more books. I guess I should have." I shook my head. I had always thought I was so smart. But faced with different problems, I wasn't so sure.

"Cheer up," Kevin said. "You've got the ability to find a way to get along and to make the best of things."

"Well, thanks," I said, even though being a smart person seemed better than just being able to get along.

17

The farther we walked, the more people we began to see. Mountains appeared in the distance, with peaks covered by snow and fog. Away from the river miners were building small tent cities. The streams alongside the trail were full of miners scooping up water and gravel and shaking it in a tool the size and shape of a frying pan. They stared at us as we walked by, and every so often, one would call out a greeting. It wasn't long before Malachi demanded we stop and try our luck.

"We don't have a pan," I said.

Malachi scowled at me. "I knew we should have brought equipment like everybody else."

"Will you just stop your incessant complaining!" Kevin suddenly said. "I don't know why Molly puts up with you."

Malachi shut his mouth and stormed off ahead. I looked

at Kevin with surprise. I had never seen him lose his temper before.

"I imagine it should be easy enough to buy a pan," I said.

Early next morning we came to a man by himself in the river. We stood watching him for a while, and then I went up to him. "Know where we can find one of those pans?"

The miner pushed his hat back off his forehead. "Nothing special about this pan. Any cooking skillet would do. But if you have a hankering for this one, why, I'm going back to Frisco. For all the luck I've had with this one, give me ten dollars and it's yours."

When the man saw that I looked surprised at the amount, he quickly added, "And it's cheap at that price. You'd pay a lot more farther up, where the mining is supposed to be better."

Kevin sighed, pulled some bills out of his pocket, and counted out the money. "Are the pickings better at Sonora?" he asked.

"It's a matter of luck." The miner handed Kevin the pan and pocketed the money. "I'm standing knee high in freezing water getting nothing but a few grains, and some bloke who hardly got his boots wet pulls out a rock the size of my fist. And I can't see any differences to where he was standing. Like I said, it's all luck. You people just arrive?"

When Kevin nodded, the miner said, "Well, good luck to you. As far as I'm concerned, I should have listened to my wife. She said I was daft to think gold would be here for the taking. I'm an educated man, but my brain must have turned to mush thinking I could make a fortune. Slow and steady, that's what my wife kept saying. Not haring after dreams. So I'm going home." He looked around. "Although I have to admit, this is tempting country."

Kevin and I were listening carefully, but Malachi was getting impatient with all this talk. He grabbed the pan out of Kevin's hand and jumped into the stream. I saw him gasp as the cold water splashed up on him. He plunged the pan into the water, and then when he started to shake it, water and gravel spilled over the sides.

"There ain't anything here," he said, looking into the pan. "Where's the gold?"

"You're being too rough, son. Be gentle. See, you swirl the water around and then you let the water sort of slop over the sides. The gold is heavier and should stay in the bottom." The miner took the pan from Malachi's hand and dipped it into the water. When he brought it up, he swirled and rocked the pan so that gravel and water splashed over the sides. Kevin and Rosalie and I gathered around watching him. Then the miner showed us the pan. In the bottom, along with what was left of the gravel, were tiny glittering flakes.

Malachi stuck his finger in. "Gold!"

"Not worth my time or yours. That isn't even a dollar. It's a hard life, son, but it's your choice. Well, I'm off to get my things together, and I'll be away." He waved at us as he left.

While Kevin and Rosalie and I ate breakfast—more beans and tortillas—Malachi stayed out in the stream dipping and shaking the pan. Out of the corner of my eye, I could see he was getting angry. He finally stomped over and picked his tortilla out of the frying pan and poured himself some coffee.

"There's no gold here," he said.

"Try a little patience," Kevin said. "But I think we should keep going. The closer it gets to spring, the more people will be arriving in San Francisco, and they're going to start coming up here. The more people, the less gold for us."

We packed up, loaded Ben, refilled our water jugs, and continued on our way. We were four days on the trail. As we neared the mountains, the trees were taller and the trail rougher. Occasionally, off to one side or the other, we would see a house or even a small farm. Once, we stopped and bought fresh bread and milk from a Mexican family. Rosalie talked to them. When she returned, she explained to Kevin what they had told her.

Kevin reported that no one at the farm remembered anybody called Malarkey. "But that doesn't mean anything. Your father might not have stopped there. Rosalie also said something about the gringos fighting with the Mexicans and throwing them out and that Sonora is a dangerous place."

"Who are gringos?" I said.

"Us," Kevin said. "Americans and Europeans. Unfortunately, a lot of our countrymen are acting like they own the gold and the rivers too."

"I'm sure my father was one of those Americans," I said.

Whenever we stopped to eat or for the night, Malachi would grab the pan and wade out into a stream. He never had any luck.

"He's doing it wrong," Kevin said. "He's spilling an awful lot of water. But I'd rather not say anything. Malachi doesn't take criticism well."

"At least it's keeping him out of trouble," I said.

The closer we got to the goldfields, the more people we saw. Some were carrying all their own luggage, others had a train of donkeys, and a few had servants and slaves doing the carrying. Some were friendly and willing to share their food or coffee with us. Once or twice a number of us would build one large fire and cook whatever food we had, including the game that some of them had shot. When there was a large group of us, Kevin didn't worry about staying awake to guard us.

Others weren't so friendly. When they passed us, they made sure we saw that they had rifles. And when they saw Rosalie, they made crude remarks and a few tried to grab her. Even Malachi came to her defense, telling the men to shut up.

"I told you we needed a rifle," he said.

"No," I said. "If they saw we had guns, they would decide we wanted to fight. They really wouldn't shoot unarmed people."

"Who says that?" Malachi said.

"We've gone this far without rifles. Unless we're threatened, I don't think we need to go out and buy one," Kevin said.

The first place we came to that seemed to be a settlement was called Wood's Creek. As in Stockton and San Francisco, there were one or two wooden buildings, but most of the dwellings were tents.

As we entered the camp, I could feel the miners' eyes on us. I wished Rosalie were wearing men's clothes too.

"Kevin, do you think it would be safer if Rosalie was dressed like a boy? I could give her my outfit. I think the men would be more respectful to me. There seems to be a problem with miners' attitudes toward Mexicans."

"You're probably right," Kevin said. "Why don't you talk to her later?"

When Malachi saw the miners busy working the creek, he grabbed our pan. Kevin stopped him.

"We have to be careful, Malachi. Can't you see the river is crowded with men? There must be some way they have that shows who has a claim to a section of the river. We can't just start anywhere. Men will think we're stealing."

"Nobody owns the river. Who's going to stop me?"

"Just slow down," I said. "We'll find a place to camp, and then we can ask around. One more day won't matter."

After finding an empty spot to camp, we tied Ben to a tree and unloaded our luggage. When we saw a man passing by, Kevin went up to him.

"Is it all right if we camp here?"

The man shrugged. "Don't look like anybody has staked it out."

"How do you stake something out?" I asked.

"Leave your stuff," the man said. "Where you're panning, same thing. You leave your tools. Nobody registers his claim, less'n he's found something. If you folks don't have a tent, though, you're going to be mighty cold tonight, what with the rain, the fog, or the wind. It might even snow."

We had felt the nights getting colder all the way up. I didn't look forward to being cold all the time now, but even more, I didn't like the idea of Rosalie and me sleeping out in the open with all those men around.

"Don't worry, folks, I think I know somebody who's planning on going back. I recollect he has a tent he might want to sell you," the man said.

"How much?" I asked.

"That's between him and you," he said. "I'll send him over."

At first the tent owner wanted a hundred dollars, but we talked him down to sixty-five. He seemed nice enough and helped us put the tent up. He even threw in his rocker.

"How's it work?" Malachi asked.

"Well, you put dirt in here. Then you keep the water running in, and you rock it back and forth, sorta like you rock a baby's cradle, and the water washes the dirt out and leaves the gold, if there is any, that is. Easier than panning. Saves your back. Some blokes have great high ones that take several men to work. This one here's small enough one man can handle it."

"I can do that. Some of the men back on the trail told me a miner found a nugget the size of a fist." Malachi grabbed the rocker.

"Just be sure nobody's claimed that spot," I said.

I left Malachi splashing around and Kevin trying to explain all over again what he should do.

Rosalie and I finished laying our things out and hanging the clothes that had gotten damp on bushes to dry. Rosalie didn't want to leave the tent. She seemed afraid. But I wanted to see what it was like to pan for gold, so I wandered down to the stream. Kevin was gone, but I saw that Malachi had left the pan by the shore so he could fool with the rocker.

I picked up the pan and waded out into the stream. Now there's cold, and *cold*, I thought. With all the tramping around in the mud and fog, not to mention what winters had been like in New Hampshire, I was used to cold, but standing in freezing water was different. I didn't mind my feet going numb, but in three seconds my hands were tingling.

I dipped the pan in the water. When Malachi looked over, he started to laugh. "Girls can't pan!" he said.

"I can do this." I swirled the water around until most of it and the gravel washed away. I looked at the bottom of the pan. Nestled in with the last of the gravel were sparkling little flakes. I scooped them out and put them into my pocket.

"I found some!" I said to Malachi, who ignored me.

I put the pan back in the water to try again.

"That ain't no job for a young lady like you," a man downstream called out to me. "It's cold and dirty work."

"Cold don't scare me none!" I called back.

Several other men gathered to watch me panning. At first I was going to yell at them to go away, but then I thought, why annoy people and cause trouble? So I pushed my hair out of my eyes and looked over with a smile.

"Seems to me it's a lot like flipping flapjacks," I said.

"The little lady has a point!" one yelled. "I'll pay you more gold than you'll find in that stream if you cook me up a mess of flapjacks."

"I'll pay you too," another yelled.

"I don't have any flour," I said, "and I don't have enough pans."

"Little lady, if you'll agree to cook, we'll get you anything you need. None of us has had a decent meal in weeks."

"I came to find gold," I wanted to say, but then I thought better of it. If there was an easier way to make money, why should I freeze to death for a few grains of gold?

I waded out of the water.

"Giving up?" Malachi called after me.

"You need to be slow and gentle," I said to him. "You'll break that contraption if you keep handling it so rough."

The man who had suggested that I cook came up to me holding his hat in his hand. "My name's Hank," he said, "and I want you to know the men are mighty grateful to you. Now you just tell me what you need, and we'll find it."

"I need flour," I said. "And shortening, and some salt

and sugar. Oh, and I need some kind of a table to work on and maybe some kindling for a fire. And don't forget more pans."

I went back to our tent and pulled off my new boots. I put them next to the tent and hoped the thin sunlight that was breaking through the clouds would dry them without shrinking them. I wiggled my bare toes.

Rosalie, who had stayed in the tent, came out to help me clear a space to work. When men brought the table and started digging for the fireplace, she ducked back into the tent. I shook my head and smiled, trying to show her there was nothing to be afraid of.

"Here's some starter," Hank said, handing me a cup with some gray stuff in it that seemed to be bubbling.

"What is it?" I said.

"Add it to the flour. It works like yeast. Friend gave it to me. You just keep adding flour to it. Lasts forever."

I nodded.

When Hank saw Rosalie covering her face with her shawl, he said, "She's skittish, ain't she? But some haven't treated them Mexicans real well. The minute any of them makes a strike, why somebody goes and runs them off and steals their claim. It ain't right, and I don't blame her for being shy. I know a little Spanish—do you think I could talk to her?"

"I wouldn't go too close," I said. "But, yes, please tell her she's safe here." I looked at him. "She *is* safe here?"

"Ma'am, I will make it my duty that she's safe. Nobody

wants to tangle with Hank Butterfield. Is that your guitar over there?"

"No, it's Rosalie's."

"The men get mighty bored here, and I wonder if she'd like to strum a few tunes this evening. The men would be mighty generous."

"You can ask her," I said.

I went over and took one of Rosalie's hands and kept smiling and pointing at Hank. He came closer and spoke softly to her. At first she shook her head, but finally she smiled and said, "*Sí.*"

"I'll be seeing you later then," Hank said.

When Kevin came back and saw me cooking, and a line of men, plates in hand, waiting outside our tent, he burst out laughing.

"Molly, Molly, you'll never starve! I swear you can find a job anywhere."

"If I can't find them, I make them," I said. "I can't believe what the men are paying me to cook a few measly flapjacks. And even Rosalie has a job. Hank talked her into entertaining them tonight with her guitar. Pa's letter said Matt had married a singer, so I guess maybe she can sing too, but we've hardly heard her talk. I hope she can make money. Matt and Pa cheated her, and I feel bad about that."

"You can't keep trying to clean up after your folks all the time," Kevin said. "And you can't protect Malachi forever. It's not helping him, you know."

"If I don't, who will? It's my family, and I'm stuck with them."

Kevin shrugged and went into the tent. I could hear him talking to Rosalie.

Hank's starter did make fluffy pancakes, but they had a sharp, tart taste. I tried to give back to Hank what I hadn't used, but he shook his head.

"I only gave you part of mine," he said. "Just keep feeding it with flour. It never goes bad. It's called sourdough starter."

When the last of the men had eaten, Rosalie, her head hanging down, came out. The men yelled and whistled. For a minute I thought she was going to run back into the tent, but then she put her head up and stared at the crowd. Kevin lifted her onto my work table and handed her the guitar.

Rosalie plucked a few notes and then started to sing softly. When she saw that the men weren't going to hurt her, she smiled and her voice became clearer. The men, who had been talking and yelling, quieted down. Rosalie had a beautiful voice, and once she started singing, I realized she had sung in public before. She knew how long to wait for the applause after a song and when to start another. Pretty soon she swayed with the music, and her feet tapped to the melody.

"I wouldn't worry about Rosalie," Kevin whispered to me.

I decided she probably wouldn't need my boys' clothes after all.

I watched in amazement as the men started throwing gold nuggets at her. After she finished, I helped her gather them up. When she went back into the tent, I didn't follow her. I didn't want to know where she kept her earnings. I wanted her to keep trusting us.

When Malachi saw the gold that Rosalie and I were getting, he said, "Why should you get all this? I'm the one who's out in that cold stream freezing to death."

"Leave your sister alone," Kevin replied.

"If you want to cook, cook," I said. "And if you paid attention to what you were doing, maybe you'd find gold. But even if you did, chances are you'd just gamble it away."

In the morning, outside the tent, I found a sack of flour, some eggs, dried beef, and a can of coffee. Before I could pick them up, a line was forming.

"Rosalie," I called, "you better get up. I think we're running a restaurant."

By the third day Rosalie and I were cooking morning, noon, and night. It was pure profit since the men supplied the food. Rosalie was also singing and even dancing at night. Malachi had given up trying to find gold. He claimed there was nothing there at all except a few crummy flakes, and if anybody did find some, they were either cheating or incredibly lucky, and everybody knew he wasn't lucky. He started to hang out at the drinking and gambling tent down the road.

After a week, I was worried. "I think it's time we moved

on," I said to Kevin one morning as we watched the sun rise. "Nobody's heard of Pa here."

"Do you really think your father has struck gold?" Kevin said.

"Probably not," I said. "But he did ask for Malachi, and I don't know, I just feel I have to find him." I swallowed hard to keep from crying. "Besides, Malachi is gambling again."

Kevin threw up his arms in disgust, but he agreed we should push on. He went to wake Malachi and started breaking camp.

I thought Rosalie might not want to leave, but she seemed happy enough to pack up her things. In an hour we had loaded up Ben, who looked the better for a week's rest. The men gave us some of their food supply, and they wouldn't accept any payment in return.

"There's Jim Town next, just before Sonora. You might want to stop there first," Hank said. "See if you can find out what's happening in Sonora. I hear there's been trouble with the Mexicans. And if you ever want to come back here, why, you'll always be welcome."

As we started off, Kevin leaned over. "For a minute, I thought that Hank was going to ask you to marry him."

"You're making fun of me," I said.

I looked back and was surprised to see Hank standing in the road staring after me.

18

"Can't you smell spring?" Kevin said as we were hiking to the next camp. "Unfortunately that's not good. It means in a few weeks there'll be hordes of men swarming over the mines."

I looked around. I was used to winter in the East, where all the trees lost their leaves and the ground was covered with snow and nothing was green. But here the trees, at least most of them, hadn't lost their leaves. Ahead I could see mountains whose tops were still capped with snow. But the air did feel softer and warmer. The trail was slowly winding up, and trees and shrubs crowded near. In the fields, weeds and small yellow flowers were beginning to appear.

"We shouldn't have stayed so long at Wood's Creek," Malachi said. "Last year they found a huge nugget there. They said it was worth thousands of dollars. But this year nobody has found anything. That's what everybody keeps saying—last year there was tons of gold, this year nothing."

"Stop complaining," I said. "Rosalie and I earned more money cooking and singing than you did panning for gold. I don't know why you want to keep doing it. It only makes you mad."

"That's because I didn't find no gold. But I know I'll find some nearer the mountains. Men told me it washes down from where the rivers start. That's what's so exciting. It's like I never know what's going to happen," Malachi said.

"Like gambling?" Kevin said.

"What d'you mean?" Malachi said. "It's not the same at all. I gamble 'cause I like beating people. It just shows them I'm not stupid like they think I am."

"I don't think you're stupid," Kevin said. "Lazy maybe."

"Shoot, I'm not lazy. Why, I stay up all night gambling," Malachi said. "And I don't mind panning, 'cause I don't have to talk to nobody."

Malachi never was much of a talker. Back home, he had hung out with the Grisson boys, who were always busy making trouble. But I don't think I ever heard them and Malachi exchange two words. That was probably why Malachi didn't like school much. If the teacher called on him, he would always mutter that he didn't know the answer. Pa should have let him stay in school, I thought. Maybe there Malachi would have learned to speak up and not have taken to gambling to prove he was smart. Sometimes I think Pa liked keeping us all stupid. Then we wouldn't argue with him.

"Do you think Pa has found any more gold?" Malachi asked.

"I just hope he still has the gold he started with," I said.

The road was rougher now, and sometimes we wandered away from the streams running down from the mountains. But every time we came to water, we found men busy panning. We asked each of them if they knew somebody called Malarkey. Most of them shook their heads and barely stopped working.

Finally, one man did give us some news. "Why do you want to know?" he asked.

Before I could tell him he was my father, Kevin quickly replied, "We heard he made a strike."

The man laughed. "Not likely. Where did you hear that? Probably one of his tall tales. I don't believe that man ever spoke a word of truth in his life."

"So you did meet him?" At least he was alive, I told myself.

"To my grief," the man replied. "He and that boy that was with him jumped another man's claim, and then they bragged about it. We ran him out of the camp, but not before he stole from just about everybody. The last thing he did was to salt a mine and sell it to some greenhorn."

"Salt a mine?" Malachi asked.

"He put some flakes of gold and a few nuggets in the water and pretended he had just found it. Got the greenhorns all excited, and then he offered to sell the spot and this idiot bought it. Everybody knew there weren't nothing in that place."

"Do you know where he went?" I said.

"Oh, he was a big talker. Told me he was going up in the mountains to find the source of all the gold. Claims he heard there was a hidden river that could hardly flow, it was so stuffed with gold. He said a man gave him a map showing him where it was. Bunch of hogwash if you ask me, just so much talk. Don't know exactly what mountains he was talking about."

"Which way would he go?"

The man stared at me. "Why are you so anxious to find him?"

"He cheated us too," Kevin quickly said.

"Not surprised. Well, I imagine he'd be heading up through Sonora. The snow should be melting by now and the pass open. Wouldn't be surprised if he left a trail easy enough to follow. I would think he stole from everybody he met."

"How far is Sonora?" Kevin asked.

"Not far—half a day's walk. Well, maybe not, seeing as you have young ladies."

Kevin snorted, and I replied, "We've been walking for months. I can walk as far and as fast as any man."

The man shook his head and went back to digging. I could hear him muttering something about how ladies weren't what they used to be and that his mother would be positively scandalized.

Some of the camps we passed had just a few men with maybe a tent or two, but one camp had become almost a town with several wooden buildings. There was a bar and another building had a sign calling itself the Jamestown Restaurant. We stopped there for food. It was greasy, and the biscuits were like rocks.

"Don't mention you could do better," Malachi said, "or we'll never get out of here."

Kevin suggested we not mention Pa, either. I agreed. If one of his victims thought we knew him, they might think we were his partners, and in a town this size we'd be hopelessly outnumbered.

"How far to Sonora?" Kevin asked the cook.

"A mile or so. But it'll be dark before you get there, and I wouldn't advise going in the dark. That town is trouble." He nodded toward Rosalie. "Have you kidnapped her?"

"Of course not," I said.

"Well, I'd be careful bringing her into Sonora. Some of them Mexicans are pretty protective about their womenfolk, and they might wonder what you're doing with one of their women."

"She wanted to come with us," I said.

"They could think you'd made her say that. But you folks don't have to pay me no never mind. Do as you please. I am just trying to help."

"He's probably right," Kevin said after the man went back to work. "Daytime would be better."

We pitched our tent outside of town. We tethered Ben, and then I had to talk Malachi out of trying to find a card game.

"It's not safe," I said. "Those men won't trust us, and if they find out we're related to Pa, well, they might just try to run us out and keep what they want of our stuff."

Malachi grumbled, but he finally agreed to stay in the tent. We all rolled up in our blankets and went to sleep.

It rained during the night, but it was a soft rain and by midmorning it had stopped and the sun was coming out. We repacked Ben, ate the food left over from dinner, and started up the trail to Sonora.

Apart from the fact that Rosalie might find her family there, I began to wonder why we were even going to Sonora. Pa had likely moved on to follow that crazy dream of a golden river. He didn't seem to stay long at any one place. Maybe we would never find him. The map he had sent us made no sense. At home it had seemed simple enough, but this was a big country, and gold could be found almost any-where. The map had no names, and the marks that seemed to show mountains and rivers could be any mountain or river. We had just been guessing all along.

I wished I could talk to Rosalie. But I couldn't seem to learn another language. Foreign words just rolled right out of my mind. By now, Kevin's Spanish was pretty good, but Rosalie didn't want to talk to him unless he asked her something directly. Most of the time she just answered by shaking or nodding her head. Perhaps at Sonora, where Rosalie would have her own people around her, she might not be so afraid of Malachi and Kevin.

I wondered how Matt and she had talked. I had never figured Matt as being smart enough to learn another language, but there were things about Malachi I hadn't realized, either. I was beginning to think I didn't know any of my brothers very well.

Sonora appeared to be more of a real town than the other camps we had passed. It had tents, of course, but also more wooden buildings. The town wandered over a series of small hills. The landscape was very different now. For quite a while after we left Stockton, the ground had been flat with bushy trees and grasses that stayed green from the rain. But now, mixed in with the short trees were tall ones with a sharp odor. They had pointed needles instead of leaves. The ground around them was covered with these needles.

We cautiously entered the town. All the rumors we had heard about the attitudes toward Mexicans and the troubles scared me. My heart jumped in fright when a large man came around from one of the tents and stopped to stare at us. Suddenly Rosalie, who was trailing behind as usual, ran forward.

"Tío Diego!" she cried.

"Rosalie!" he shouted. He flung his arms around her.

Rosalie seemed to change into a different person. She almost sparkled, and she was talking so fast, even her uncle raised his hands, laughed, shook his head, and then put his finger on her lips. By this time, a crowd of men and a few women were gathering around trying to hug Rosalie. Her uncle came over to us.

"Which one of you is her husband?" he asked Kevin and Malachi. "We heard she was married."

"You speak English?" I asked.

"*Sí*, but not well. Which one is her husband?"

"Neither one." I spoke slowly. "We heard Rosalie had married my brother, but we don't know where my father and brother are. They seem to have gone off."

The uncle frowned. "Are you sure they were married?"

"No," I said. "We weren't there."

"This is not a good thing," the uncle said. "This is very bad. How do we know she was not taken advantage of?"

I shook my head. "We weren't there," I repeated. "And we aren't sure what happened."

"Yes, I am not blaming you. It was good of you to bring her to us. For that, thank you. My name is Diego Vasquez. I am pleased to meet you."

Watching Rosalie with all her family, I suspected this was where she had wanted to go all along. I doubt if she really wanted to find Matt. I think she just wanted to be with her relatives. Matt and Pa could have gone in the opposite direction in their hunt for the river of gold. They could have told the men along the way they were going to Sonora to fool them.

Uncle Diego went over to Rosalie and asked her questions. When she began to cry, some of the young men gave us angry looks. Then I could see Rosalie shaking her head. She seemed to be saying something in our defense.

Soon Uncle Diego came back over. "Rosalie says you have been very kind. It would be our pleasure if you would eat with us." He gestured to a large table that was set under a tree outside their tent. The food smelled wonderful.

Malachi immediately sat himself at the table.

One of the women gently led me over and pushed me down on a stool next to him.

The table was heaped with food: bowls of beans, a skillet with some kind of meat, and piles of tortillas. Malachi filled his plate and immediately started eating, his head almost touching the plate.

"Malachi!" I said. "You're eating like an animal. Sit up."

"I'm hungry. This is good."

The younger women were looking at Malachi, giggling and poking each other.

No one else started to eat until Uncle Diego bowed his head and said a prayer. It had been a long time since we had such good food. I allowed the women to fill my plate more than once. When we had finished, Uncle Diego sat down beside me.

"You are most welcome to stay with us," he said. "But I must warn you, it could be dangerous. If the gringos come, they won't hurt you if you are alone, but if they see you with us, they might become very angry and throw you out too."

"Why are they doing that?" I said.

"Because many gringos think this is their land and all the gold should belong to them," Kevin explained.

"He is right," Uncle Diego said. "Once this was our land, and then one day our flag was taken down and the red, white, and blue flag was flying, and now we are not welcome here. So we are leaving. There is gold here and they want it, so we are moving on. It is not worth our people dying. If there is gold here, there will be gold somewhere else and we will find it."

"When are you going?" I asked.

Uncle Diego shrugged. "My cousin and his son are mining down in the valley, and they listen to what is happening. They will tell us if people are talking trouble, and then we will be gone. It was good of you to care for Rosalie and we are grateful, but I do not think we can protect you if you stay with us." He paused. "But don't worry now—finish your meal, and whatever happens, happens." He shook Kevin's shoulder. "So, my friend, eat with us, but sleep in your own tent and all will be well."

When he had left, I turned to Kevin. "Should we stay here?"

"Maybe for a while," he said. "I don't think we have anything to worry about with the Mexicans right now. I think Rosalie's uncle is a leader. The real problem is, we're gringos, and if there's trouble, then Uncle Diego is right. He might not be able to control his group. But let's not panic. It seems to be quiet now, and we're safe for the time being. But I don't think we can stay here too long."

Uncle Diego came back and said to me, "My wife and sisters want to know if you are wearing boy's clothes because you have lost your own. If so, they will give you a dress to wear."

I laughed. "No, I have dresses in my luggage. But I would like to wash my clothes if that is possible."

"Of course. The women would be glad to help you. Come along. You can use our tent."

Inside the tent I pulled out one of my dresses. It was wrinkled, but it didn't smell as bad as the clothes I was wearing. I pulled them off and dropped them into a heap and put on the dress. When the women saw me, they laughed and patted my skirt.

"*Sí, sí,*" they said.

I was going to wash my clothes in the river, but the women led me behind their tent where they had set up a sort of laundry. They had a fire going and a large pot with water. After I had scrubbed my clothes, I hung them on bushes to dry. Since I couldn't understand a word the women were saying, I was soon restless from sitting with them. So I decided to wander around the town. Some of the men stared at me, and a few made threatening gestures. But I really didn't think they would attack a woman. Seeing their reaction, though, made me wonder what could happen to Malachi— or Kevin for that matter. I returned to the campsite and found Kevin putting up our tent.

"Where's Malachi?"

"He left with the rocker."

"He's going to get into trouble," I said. "I just feel it, and when he does, even Rosalie's uncle won't be able to save us."

"I guess you want me to go find him," Kevin said.

"No, that's okay." I hated always asking Kevin to watch out for Malachi.

"Never mind, I'll go," he replied.

When Kevin came back, he said Malachi seemed to be keeping himself busy panning for gold. Later in the day Rosalie came over and smiled and gestured for us to join them for the evening meal. Malachi wandered back. He was pleased and excited because he had several small nuggets in his hand.

Uncle Diego looked at them. "Good," he said. "Five dollars, maybe ten."

"Better than farming," Malachi said.

I didn't point out that he had wasted plenty of time not finding anything. It was nice to see him in a good humor. He sat next to the younger men, and after eating, they shoved their stools back and got up and went off. Malachi followed them.

Uncle Diego shook his head. "Young men," he said. "They can be so foolish."

"Where are they going?" I said.

"Play monte and drink," he said.

"Monte?"

"A card game," Kevin answered.

"There goes his gold," I said.

"He's a big boy," Kevin replied.

"Not really."

I lay awake that night waiting for Malachi to come back. I could hear Kevin across the tent snoring lightly. I remembered what Mr. Dorset had said about people getting the wrong idea about Kevin and me. I hoped Rosalie's family thought he was a cousin or something.

It was almost dawn when I heard Malachi stumble into the tent. He was grumbling to himself, something about stupid foreign games and how was he supposed to know the rules. But he was up early in the morning, carrying the rocker under his arm. He grabbed a few tortillas off the Vasquezes' table and headed off with some of the other men.

When my pants and shirt were dry, I put them back on despite the giggles of Rosalie and her friends.

"I'm going to try panning," I said. After all, this was what I was supposed to have come for, and I had to return some of Mrs. Throckmorton's money. I wondered if she would have given me the money if she had known I would earn most of it by cooking and ironing. I carried our pan. I certainly wasn't going to try and take the rocker away from Malachi.

The streams were full from the winter rains, but as Kevin explained to me, when the snow started to melt high up in the mountains, there was always the danger of floods. Some of the riverbeds were damp with no running water in them, because, with all the digging and damming the miners had done, the rivers had changed course. So I could either find a place in the water, or I could dig in the abandoned beds and carry the dirt to the water and wash it there.

I decided I'd rather dig and walk than stand in freezing water and listen to the men make fun of me.

It was hard work. The dirt was heavy, and I still had to get wet running water over the pan and then shaking it. It was boring and dirty, and after a while my hands were blistered and bloody. But just when I was thinking about giving up, I saw something glittering in the bottom of my pan. I reached in and pulled out a nugget—not flakes, but a nugget. I bent down and washed it more carefully. I hoped it was real gold. I shoved it into my pocket and trudged back to the spot where I had gotten the dirt.

I skipped lunch. I didn't want to stop now that I had found something. By the time the light was beginning to fade, I had five nuggets. When I got back to camp, I showed them to Kevin. I tried not to get too excited.

"Well done," Kevin said. "It certainly looks like the real thing."

"What's it worth?"

"Ask Uncle Diego."

Diego weighed them in his hand. "Seventy-five dollars, maybe," he said. "You have made a strike."

"What will you do with it?" Kevin said.

I looked at them. Seventy-five dollars was a lot of money. I had told Mrs. Throckmorton I would send her half of my earnings.

"I guess I could return the loan or part of it. I should have written Mrs. Throckmorton when we were in San Francisco. Don't tell Malachi I found any gold."

"Why, Molly," Kevin said, "don't you trust Malachi?"

I ignored his gibe. "No matter what I do, he never stops wasting his money and running around with troublemakers."

"Well, that's really his choice," Kevin said. "You're not his mother, you know."

For the next few days it was quiet in the camp. I went panning every day. Kevin said I should have staked my claim, but I knew the men wouldn't respect it because I was a girl, so each day I worked a different spot.

One day Diego came to me. "What do you know of the marriage of my niece and that brother of yours?"

I sighed. Did Diego think I was hiding something? "I don't know anything," I said. "We are Catholics, but I don't think Matt would worry about finding a priest to marry them. Doesn't Rosalie have any papers? A license or something?"

"She has nothing. I mean your family no disrespect, but I am wondering if your brother was tricking her and that maybe there is no legal marriage."

"I wouldn't be surprised," I replied.

"We will soon be going back to Mexico, and I will ask the officials to look into the matter. It would not be right that Rosalie can never marry again and have a family. I don't think we will ever find that brother of yours, and begging your pardon, I suspect he might not tell the truth. And it is better that Rosalie's cousin and uncles do not find him. I cannot control the younger men. I must also tell you, there are rumors that many gringos have heard this is a place rich in gold."

I remembered his words when I woke up the next day to find the Vasquez family gone. They had left a pile of tortillas at our tent and a bowl of beans. Not all the Mexicans had left, but now, without their protection, we worried about how the other Mexicans might feel about us. Even Malachi showed some sense and didn't go out playing monte with the remaining young men.

"We have to leave," Kevin said.

"Where will we go?"

"It's up to you. We can keep looking for your father and brother, or . . ." He shrugged.

"Don't you care where we go?"

"Not really," Kevin replied. "I am having my adventure. I've learned a lot, and I've met interesting people. I never really came out to find gold."

"Let's go back to San Francisco," I suddenly said.

"Good. Shall we leave tomorrow?" Kevin replied.

I told Malachi we were going back to San Francisco the next day. I thought he would argue with me, but he only grunted.

When I woke up the next morning, Malachi was gone.

19

Besides his clothes Malachi had taken the rocker and Ben. I was glad I had stuffed my leather pouch holding my gold nuggets under my head at night, but I was angry he had taken Ben, a gentle, patient little animal. I was afraid Malachi wouldn't treat him well. I hoped he would sell Ben to someone kind, but I doubted he would even think about that. When he was through with Ben, he would give him to whoever gave him the best price.

"Trust Malachi to just go off and leave us stranded," Kevin said. He kicked at our belongings piled in the middle of the tent. "We can't carry all this stuff."

I looked over my things: my clothes, the blanket I slept in, the pan for the gold. And my quilt, which was ragged and torn, but I knew I couldn't leave it. Kevin had a similar pile. And then there were the cooking things we had gathered along the way: the coffee pot and other pans the men from Wood's Creek had given me.

"Can't we throw something away?" Kevin said.

"I need what I have," I said. I hadn't dragged my dresses and quilt for miles only to leave them here. "Couldn't we buy another horse?"

"I'll see if anybody will sell us one," Kevin said.

Late in the day he came back leading a fuzzy burro with soft brown eyes.

"Oh, he's sweet." I rubbed his nose. "What did he cost?"

"Twenty-five dollars."

"I guess that's fair. Were the Mexicans nice?"

"Well, they didn't threaten me," Kevin said. "But I don't see any reason to hang around any longer. If the American miners arrive, there could be fighting, and frankly they might think you're a dance hall girl and take advantage of you."

I looked down at the pants and shirt I was wearing. "If they think I'm a dance hall girl, they must be blind."

It was still light, and there was no reason to stay, so we started down. We were not alone on the trail. The men coming down from the mines fell into two groups. There were those who had struck gold and were bringing it down to be weighed and exchanged for cash. They were suspicious and kept to themselves. Many of them had guns. The others were like us, just going back. Some of them were sick with terrible coughs; almost all complained that they had left their families for nothing. They were friendly enough, though, and we often ate dinner with them. But they did a lot of whining, and we didn't stay together as a group. Most of us traveled at different speeds. Some even stopped to try panning.

The weather was getting warmer now and the green meadows were beginning to turn golden yellow. Some of the meadows were filled with bright orange flowers. When we stopped for the night, Kevin slept outside the tent.

"The insects are terrible," I said. "And it still isn't that warm at night. You can sleep in the tent, I don't mind."

"I do," said Kevin. "This arrangement could cause talk."

"If it doesn't bother me, I don't see why it should bother anyone else." None of the men had ever questioned what my relationship to Kevin and Malachi had been. But maybe Kevin was right and I was just being foolish thinking that appearances didn't matter.

The trip down to Stockton went quickly. We didn't stop to pan for gold, and we ate only two meals a day. The settlements we passed were larger now, just a few weeks later, and there seemed to be more of them. At night we would try to judge whether the miners in them were friendly. If they waved and called out to us or asked us questions, we would stop and spend the night there. Most of the men were willing to sell us food and were eager to hear what the mines farther east were like and how much gold we had found. I just said some people were finding gold, but since the snow hadn't melted yet, the only water in the streams came from the winter rains.

If we passed a town where the men were armed or

grunted if we tried to talk to them, we kept moving. On such nights we would be sure to find a place to sleep that was away from the main trail.

I couldn't believe what had happened to Stockton in the time we had been away. The harbor was crowded with boats and ships of all kinds, and there were now more wooden buildings than tents. There was even a raised wooden sidewalk, and the men were able to push wheelbarrows along it and avoid the mud in the street. Many of the buildings were stores. I peered into one and found it was selling everything a person would need: cans of food, clothes, shoes, and gold pans. The docks reminded me of Boston, with crates and barrels being unloaded.

Bill's pub had been turned into a fancy restaurant with tables and white tablecloths, and the choices of food were written on pieces of paper that were pasted on the window. When we entered the restaurant, I could see some of the men looking at us and nudging each other. I couldn't blame them. Both Kevin and I were dirty. We headed to the kitchen to see if we could find Bill.

He was so busy handing dishes to the waiters, he barely glanced up when we came in.

"Out, out!" he ordered. "This is a kitchen."

"Don't you want to hear about Rosalie?" I asked.

"Rosalie?" He looked at us more closely. "Of course, how stupid of me. You are the sister of the man who seduced her. Is she safe?"

"She's with her family," I said.

"Did she find your brother?"

"No, but her uncle is taking care of her," I said.

"Good. Sit down." Bill gestured to the man who was washing the dishes. "Clear a space for my friends. So tell me, did you find gold? What is it like up in the mines?"

"Oh, there's a little gold," I said. "But it's hard work getting it."

"Of course it is. What do people expect?" Bill said. "Where are you off to now—or are you planning to settle here?"

"We're going back to San Francisco," I said.

"And then home? Back east?"

I didn't answer. I didn't know.

The men who had been lucky left their nuggets and flakes with assayers in Stockton, who tested the gold to see how much it was worth. If the men decided to go back to the mines, they often left their money with the assayers, who acted as a bank. Or they had it sent back home.

I wasn't ready to have my gold tested. If it didn't turn out to be worth much, I didn't want to know right away. I'd have it tested in San Francisco. The next morning we sold our donkey to Bill and thanked him for letting us sleep in his storeroom again.

It was much easier going back to San Francisco than it had been getting to Stockton. Once the cargo had been unloaded from their boats, the captains were more than happy to take us back. We now found ourselves sharing space with the miners who had failed. The ship was crowded, although not as badly as it had been coming up here. And since on this ship there was no load of lumber taking up the hold, many of the miners slept there.

"Makes you think men are just going back and forth," I said to Kevin as we stored our luggage on the deck. "Even the ones who find a little bit of gold are going back."

"Like you?" Kevin asked.

"Like me," I agreed.

Except for the mosquitoes and other flying bugs, the trip down was quiet. The river and bays were filled with water, so there was little danger of us being caught on a sandbar, and there was no rain.

"Not likely to see much more rain now," the captain said. "By the end of the summer things will be pretty dry."

If Stockton had grown, San Francisco had exploded. Everywhere we looked there were sturdy wooden buildings and cobbled streets. Most of the tents were gone from the downtown area and were now in the hills and out near the streams. Some of the docked ships were being used as offices with signs hanging from their sides. The captain of our boat had to moor far out in the bay, and his crewmen rowed us to the shore.

"It's a sorry thing to see ships being treated like that," a sailor said. "Letting landlubbers use them. Disgrace, if you ask me."

"Why do they do it?" I said.

"Nobody left on board. Everybody jumped ship. Can't sail a ship alone. So they just sit there rotting."

It seemed to me using them for offices was better than letting them fall apart.

Once we were on shore, we were totally lost. Nothing was the same. I wasn't even sure where Mrs. Parnell's house was.

"This is scary."

"Come on, there's a restaurant over there," Kevin said.

"It looks too stuck up," I replied. It had a fancy awning over the door, and one of the windows had colored glass in it. "There's another one across the street. That doesn't look so fancy. Look at us, we're a mess."

"Molly, it doesn't matter how we're dressed. Look at the people on the street," he said.

Of course, he was right. Men in satin vests, Chinese with long pigtails swinging down their backs, men dressed like us in dirty mining clothes, and women in bright ruffled dresses with pink spots on their cheeks and hair piled high on their heads were all crowding the sidewalks.

Kevin steered me into the restaurant. It was dark with brown paneling on the wall and thick red drapes and white tablecloths.

"You two want a table?" a man wearing a black suit asked.

"That will be fine," Kevin said, giving me a wink.

"There will be an hour's wait."

"Never mind." I pulled on Kevin's arm.

We went back outside. "I think we should ask where Mrs. Parnell is," I said. "I don't think those snotty people would know."

We chose a bar that advertised lunches. The place was as dark as the first one, but there were no white tablecloths and there was sawdust on the floor.

We sat down at a table.

"What are you going to do?" Kevin asked.

"Find Mrs. Parnell."

"No, Molly, you know that's not what I mean. You can't stay in San Francisco alone."

"Why not?" I tried to sound sure of myself, but inside I wasn't so sure. "Are you going back and be a doctor with your uncle?"

The waiter came over and put two heavy white china mugs in front of us and poured some coffee.

"You people want something to eat?"

"Sure, what have you got?" Kevin said.

He gestured to a blackboard on the wall.

"Eggs," I said.

Kevin nodded.

When the waiter left, I looked at Kevin. "You're not going back, are you?"

"If you were going back, I would," he replied.

"But why does what I do matter?"

"Molly, you're a girl."

"I know that," I said. "But you don't owe me anything. You don't have to take care of me."

"Maybe I want to. I've been thinking," Kevin said. "We should get married."

I sputtered into my coffee. "Married?"

I would have said more, but the waiter came and dropped our plates in front of us.

"Are you crazy?" I finally said when he left. Then I realized that sounded terrible. I looked at Kevin—he was one of the nicest people I had ever known. I thought for a minute. "I'm sorry, Kevin. I'm just surprised. I mean—"

I stopped. I didn't know what I meant. "I'm sorry. I can't answer you right now. I never thought of us being a couple or anything."

"I understand," Kevin said. "But think about it now, will you?"

"Yes." I poked at my eggs. I had lost my appetite. When the waiter returned, I asked him if he knew Mrs. Parnell.

"The Irish washerwoman? Sure, she's built a boarding-house up the hill. Near Washerwoman's Lagoon. Just go outside and turn left at the corner. Follow the road up the hill."

"She built a house in a few weeks?"

"Where you been? Things move fast here."

We left the bar and followed his directions. We were silent. I certainly didn't know what to say, and I doubted if Kevin did either. All of the easy friendship between us had disappeared.

Mrs. Parnell's house was where her old place had been. It was bigger than the other one, a sturdy two-story building, but it had a raw, unfinished look.

When Mrs. Parnell opened the door and saw us, she put her hand over her heart.

"Saints preserve us! Is that you, Molly?"

"It's me." I felt myself being enfolded in her arms. I started to cry.

"Come in, come in. Isn't this lovely? I never dreamed you would be back so soon. And just in time to see my new house. Would you even know the place?"

The ground floor was a large eating room and kitchen. Mrs. Parnell looked at Kevin. "I've started feeding my boarders. None of that fancy stuff like near the wharf. Just good, hearty cooking. The sleeping area is still out back," she said. "I have plans for the barn, but I was lucky to get this much built. The men are starting to go back to the mines. In a few weeks there won't be an able-bodied man to hire. But there are new beds and dividers to give the boarders some privacy. And I have a snug little room upstairs that you can use," she said to me. "No more sleeping on the kitchen table."

When Kevin left to go out back, Mrs. Parnell looked at me. "You're worn out. Come along. I'll fill my bathtub with warm water and you go soak."

She took me to a room in the back. She filled a long tin tub with hot water, then handed me a towel and a bar of soap. I lay in the tub for a long time. The last time I had had a good bath was in Panama. Since then I had just washed my hands and face. The streams and rivers had been too cold to bathe in.

I stretched out and watched the steam curl toward the ceiling. For a while I just rested there, but finally I began to think. Kevin was nice and I liked him, but even though we had traveled together for months, I still didn't think I really knew him. We had been too busy getting from here to there. He had been the big brother I wished I had had.

When the water started to cool down, I got out and dried myself off. I picked up my dirty clothes. I hated to put them on again, but I couldn't wander around wrapped in a towel. When Mrs. Parnell saw me, she shook her head. She had found one of my dresses and ironed it.

"I wasn't being nosy, but I knew you would need clean clothes. The ones you arrived in were a disgrace. I didn't touch anything else."

"Of course you didn't," I said. "I trust you."

She handed the dress to me and told me to run up to the little room at the left of the stairs. "I brought the rest of your things up there."

I dressed slowly. The skirts felt strange, but I found I liked the feeling against my legs. My boots were a mess, all stained with mud. I hoped they would clean up. In the house I didn't mind going barefoot.

"Why don't you go and tell Kevin he can take a bath if he wants? I've heated up more water," Mrs. Parnell suggested.

When I hesitated, Mrs. Parnell looked at me. "Trouble, eh?" she said. "Never mind, I'll do it."

When she came back, she sat down at the kitchen table. "Now then. Where is your brother?"

"Left."

"Is that what's bothering you?"

"No," I said. "I knew I couldn't watch after Malachi forever. And after we realized we would probably never find my father, I wasn't surprised he just up and left."

"That's all for the good," she said. "There was no holding that boy, and he was bringing you nothing but grief. Maybe he'll straighten up on his own. So if that's not what's bothering you, what is it?"

"It's Kevin. He asked me to marry him."

"And you don't know what to do?"

"No," I said. "I mean, yes, I don't know what to do."

"He's a good man, he's kind, and he would take care of you."

"That's the problem," I said. "I don't want to be taken care of like I'm a child or something. I want to take care of myself."

"If we were back east, I would say you were being foolish," Mrs. Parnell said. "But here a woman can be independent. Maybe that would be the right thing for you. But, Molly, don't get too independent. Being married isn't wrong. It just might be wrong for you right now."

"I guess," I said. I wondered if my grandmother had married my grandfather just because she wanted to be taken care of. If so, it hadn't worked. In the end she still had to take care of herself.

"What will you do?" Mrs. Parnell said.

"That's the trouble. I don't know."

"Do you have any money?"

"I found some gold, and I earned some more cooking for men in a camp, but I need to send most of it back to Mrs. Throckmorton. She lent me the money to come out here."

"Well, lass, send your friend some of the money, but keep some for yourself for the time being. A girl needs to have a little put aside in case things go wrong. Meanwhile, you can stay here and help me. I'll pay you a fair wage, although things will get quiet for a while, but we can always take in laundry again. In the winter when the men come back, we'll have much to do."

"Thank you," I said.

"It's nice having you here. You're like the daughter I never had," Mrs. Parnell said. "Just don't decide anything too fast."

Kevin came through the kitchen sensibly carrying his clean clothes. "Why, Miss Molly, I wouldn't recognize you. You look like a girl again."

"The pants came in handy," I said. "I'm going to keep them."

"You're not going gold panning again, are you?" he said. He looked surprised. "I thought you were through with that."

"No," I said. "It's too uncertain, and it can be a waste of

time. You never know from day to day what you'll find. And it's awfully hard work."

"I thought hard work never stopped you," Kevin teased.

"Up to a point," I said. "But if I'm going to work hard, I want something to show for it."

"Pardon me, Kevin," said Mrs. Parnell. "I have several pots of water simmering on the stove for your bath. Why don't you just empty the water from the tub into the backyard and fill it up with this fresh water?"

Kevin ignored Mrs. Parnell. "I was thinking," he said to me. "I might just start practicing medicine out here. From what we saw in the camps, I'm sure I could make a living."

"That sounds very sensible," Mrs. Parnell said. "But I need the stove for things other than boiling water. So take your bath now, and we can talk later."

I watched him go into the back room. He might have his future planned, but that was his future, not mine. I had a future—I just didn't know what it was. I could always teach school. I doubted I would need a certificate, but I wasn't sure there were enough children out here yet to make a school practical. I could cook in a restaurant, but I wasn't all that good a cook. I was okay for men who hadn't had a decent meal in weeks, but I wasn't good enough for the restaurants in San Francisco. There must be something else out there that I didn't even know about yet. It didn't really matter if I didn't find out right away. I had all the time I needed because I could take care of myself.